Overland on the Hippie Trail

by

Larry Farmer

Overland on the Hippie Trail

COPYRIGHT © 2018 by Larry Farmer

Contact Information: info@thewildrosepress.com

Cover Art by *Tina Lynn Stout*

The Wild Rose Press, Inc.
PO Box 708
Adams Basin, NY 14410-0708
Visit us at www.thewildrosepress.com

Publishing History
First Vintage Rose Edition, 2018
Print ISBN 978-1-5092-1958-2
Digital ISBN 978-1-5092-1959-9

Published in the United States of America

By Vienna, 1978, I wanted to go overland. Overland by way of what was called the Hippie Trail. India was the chic place to go, if you were a true adventurer. I still hated hippies, but I did love this about them, their free and open-road way of life, the wanting to get out of the mold, away from the rat race, and see things and places you'd only read or heard about. The Marines got me started on that, structured as it was in a war zone called Vietnam, but I loved my generation's open-road spirit and wanted to follow it too, to see these places first hand and not as a part of a group tour package of five countries in three days.

I wanted to mingle with the crowds, the locals, to eat their food and put up with the hardships, to sleep in a ditch if I must, or in some sleazy hotel. I wanted to experience the joy and pure fun of staying in exotic place after exotic place.

The Hippie Trail began in Vienna. That's why I was there. Vienna was the capital of Austria, which meant it had embassies where you could get the travel visas you needed for the Asian countries you passed through on the way to India. And Vienna was on the edge of Asia Minor, where these Asian countries began.

It seemed fitting that it was my search on the Internet for a Beatles song that reminded me indirectly of those days and of meeting Ewa. For it was the Beatles who introduced my generation to India. Not the historical India so much as the India of the new mystique.

Dedication

To the women who raised me—
my mother Lynelle, and my sisters Linda and Lawanna

Chapter 1

It's strange how so much in life intertwines, the complex networking in our brain and the way it stores and links so many of our memories.

I am a big Beatles fan, and while searching on an Internet browser for one of their love ballads, I found other artists who performed the song, in particular, a female duet from Vienna.

Vienna.

I always loved Vienna. It was the epicenter of European grandeur not all that long ago—music, art, sophistication. The Hapsburg dynasty ruled Europe's most impressive empire from there for centuries. I had an aunt belonging to that nobility, which put a personal flavor on this glory for me.

But Vienna means much more to me now. Some of my warmest memories originate from that city. For that's where I met Ewa.

Ewa spelled her name with a "w," though it is pronounced as a "v," as is the case for Germanic languages. In addition, the "e" leading in her name was pronounced as a long "a" would be in English, making her name sound like "Ava," as in Ava Gardner, the movie actress.

I first visited Vienna from Frankfurt, West Germany, in my twenties, when I worked as a civil servant for the US military in 1974. But a few years later I was back, and not just as a tourist. I was dissatisfied with my life.

The irony is that by my return to Vienna in 1978, I seemed to be living the life of the hippie subculture I thought I detested. I wore blue jeans and travelled around with a backpack as if I was one, in spite of my short, blond hair and my still traditional and patriotic outlooks to life. A hippie without the drugs, sex, or rock-and-roll, you might say. And my name set the record straight also, a very unhippie name: Hunter.

Overland.

By Vienna, 1978, I wanted to go overland. Overland by way of what was called the Hippie Trail. India was the chic place to go, if you were a true adventurer. I still hated hippies, but I did love this about them, their free and open-road way of life, the wanting to get out of the mold, away from the rat race, and see things and places you'd only read or heard about. The Marines got me started on that, structured as it was in a war zone called Vietnam, but I loved my generation's open-road spirit and wanted to follow it too, to see these places first hand and not as a part of a group tour package of five countries in three days.

I wanted to mingle with the crowds, the locals, to eat their food and put up with the hardships, to sleep in a ditch if I must, or in some sleazy hotel. I wanted to experience the joy and pure fun of staying in exotic place after exotic place.

The Hippie Trail began in Vienna. That's why I was there. Vienna was the capital of Austria, which meant it had embassies where you could get the travel visas you needed for the Asian countries you passed through on the way to India. And Vienna was on the edge of Asia Minor, where these Asian countries began.

It seemed fitting that it was my search on the Internet for a Beatles song that reminded me indirectly of those days and of meeting Ewa. For it was the Beatles who introduced my generation to India. Not the historical India so much as the India of the new mystique—meditation, incense, ashrams, the sitar, and yoga.

My memories were fresh and vivid, on one hand, and with a dreamlike surrealness on the other. How precious indeed those days were.

Chapter 2

It wasn't until I checked into the youth hostel in Vienna for the night that I noticed how lonely I felt. Even then I noticed it only because I had time to do so, now that I was settled and with plans, finished with filling out the forms for my visa processing at the Turkish and Iranian embassies. It left me time now to think. And to fret. And to wonder why I was doing all this.

I had only eight hundred dollars to my name, so there was little room for failure or misjudgment. But living on nothing half way around the world also made things more adventurous to me, which was another reason I wanted to do this, the me-against-the-world challenge I still sought since my days in the Marines.

"Hallo," a voice from behind me said.

"Hello," I returned, as the blonde girl walked with her tray of food to the end of the table in the dining room where I sat.

"You are Hunter, no?" she asked shyly. "Do you remember me from when we watched the television news program last night? We made conversation as we watched. Do you remember this event between us?"

"Of course, Ewa," I said, smiling back at her.

I was glad she remembered me enough to seek me out. I had the feeling it was meeting her the previous night that had stirred up these lonely feelings I suddenly had to deal with now. Being with her made me wish for a steadier fixture of warmth in my life. She strongly exuded warmth.

Suddenly, meeting Ewa in Vienna put a breath of fresh air into me. She was from Warsaw, Poland, the first person I'd met from the Eastern European Soviet Bloc of countries called the Warsaw Pact, which countered our NATO Bloc of Western European countries. I adored her Slavic accent. And the way she struggled at times with her English made her seem especially cute. Except that "cute" was an insult to the likes of her. She was gorgeous in her looks, especially in the knee-length dresses she wore. She had the face and figure of a Hollywood model, with long, flowing blonde hair to boot. The one flaw, if you called it that, was how short she was. I guessed her to be five foot two at the most, an entire foot shorter than my six-foot-three frame.

"May I have a seat beside you, Hunter?" she asked, still with a shy demeanor.

"Please do," I replied.

I smiled at her as she settled across from me.

"Aren't you cold?" I asked her. "It's late October, and the autumn weather is nippy. I'm wearing a sweatshirt. How can you get by in this weather in a dress with short sleeves?"

"When I go about outside, I am wearing a pullover," she explained. "But, Hunter, in Warsaw it is much more nippy than in Wien. Is that what you call this cold weather now? Nippy, you say?"

"Wien" is German for "Vienna," with the true spelling and pronunciation for the Austrian capital. The "w" again has a "v" sound, with the "e" almost silent and the "i" sounding like a long "e" would in English, forming the nearly one-syllable pronunciation.

I appreciated all the German I'd learned over the summer with my illegal job working for the *Burgermeister*, or mayor, of a small Bavarian village. They were so desperate for manual laborers to do maintenance work that I was hired through a friend I had met during the spring in Israel. The wages were good, too, for a bum like me, anyway. And the work I did on my friend's dairy farm on weekends got me a free place to stay on top of that. The village was provincial enough that hardly anyone spoke anything but German, enough so that I was forced to learn the language, and much more than I learned in Frankfurt working on a US military base. Since Ewa spoke German well, we had at first tried to converse the previous night in that. Her frustration proved enough, however, with my limited knowledge, that we soon reverted to English, which she also knew well.

Ewa's directness, mixed with her shyness, attracted me. Everything about her attracted me, actually. Especially the way she seemed to like being around me.

"How was it today for you with your visa getting, Hunter?" she asked me as she sipped at her soup.

"I never saw so many forms to fill out," I answered, letting some of my frustration show. "Do they not want us going to their countries, I wonder? I finished the papers for Turkey so late I barely managed to get into the Iranian embassy before they closed for the day. Somehow I got those papers filled out too. I feel grateful, but that's just two down. I still have Afghanistan, Pakistan, and India to go. Tomorrow's Friday. If I don't get them done tomorrow, I'll have to wait the entire weekend. Hopefully on Monday I can get my passport stamped by them all and be on my way."

"You go all the way to India, you say, Hunter? That sounds so marvelous. I fully envy you. But what a journey. I would never go there alone. Over the map, anyway. How do you say? You know, by land. The bus and train. You must be so brave, this Marine that you are. Maybe to fly to India I would go, but then you do not see the places in between like you will do with this plan of yours. Yes, I envy you. It must be exciting. You must write to me then and tell me all the wonders you behold. Okay? You will do this?"

She leaned forward to touch the pendant I was wearing.

"But you must not wear this, Hunter. This *Judenstern* you have. The Star of David. You must be more discreet about being a Jew. Many of these countries are not sympathetic to Jews."

She leaned back to sit upright with a pained expression on her face as she continued. "Especially mine, I must say, my dear fellow. We in Poland were not kind to the Jews in our history. I want to say apology words to you now for it. I hope your ancestors did not come from Poland. My conscience would not allow me to sleep now that I met someone like you. Then the worst of the Holocaust was in my country also. I know the Nazis made this holocaust and also hated the Slavs of which make up so much of my country. But it is unbearable to think of the atrocities to your people in my country."

My smile toward her was more than polite. She meant all she said. I felt bad for wearing my pendant, now that she had a guilt complex. Nor was I in the mood to feel a victim, especially at her expense. Yet her concern warmed me toward her even more.

"I got this in Israel," I explained to her. "I had an Israeli girlfriend who gave it to me. I've worn it ever since. Even after we broke up and I left, I still wear it. I love being Jewish. And this is from Israel itself, given to me by my Israeli Jewish girlfriend."

"Where is she now?" Ewa asked.

"Still in Israel."

"You were in love with her then?"

I nodded yes.

"Then why did you leave her, Hunter? You must not leave the people you love. It is as if you still love her. And you show a loss on your face to talk about it with me."

I shrugged.

"Tell me about her, Hunter."

"Where do I start?" I sighed.

"Is it so complicated?"

"Not really, but it gets so out of context. My life lately is so connected to so many things I've done. When I left home to travel, after the war in Vietnam, like I mentioned last night when we talked, I just wanted to get away. I needed answers in my life.

"Then the war broke out in Israel my first time there. I loved Israel but left it after the war, and regretted it. I lived a while in Germany, then went home to farm with my dad in Texas. He wanted me to take it over. I told him I would, but then I saw my friends moving off the farms around. A lot of them, anyway.

"I had a year of college left to get my degree, so I got it first. Then when I went to farm with my dad, I decided I didn't want to do that after all. I still felt uncomfortable in America, just like I did coming home from Vietnam. Things were changing, and even more was changing inside of me.

"Plus it was harder to farm, too. Farms are expensive, and we have to borrow a lot. Inflation was high, economic growth was stagnant, interest rates were horrible. It was getting harder to make a living, and that was with government subsidies even. A subsidy is when the government pays us to do what they want us to do about our business. In my case, farming."

She slowly nodded her head.

"Yes, I know of these government payments. We have this method in Poland also."

"Well, there are similarities with ours and what you do in Poland, but not really the same. Anyway, I left the farm again. I felt bad about it, but I left, and I still wasn't ready to live a structured life in some big city. Even with a degree in business. I was glad America was prosperous, but it just didn't attract me. Not after all I've seen and done in my life. So I have a friend back in Texas who is a writer. He had just come back from India and had an address there. I liked the idea of visiting, and especially if I go overland. So here goes."

Ewa stared at me as if digesting it all. She turned away momentarily in thought before sipping again on her soup.

Finally she said, "Yes, Hunter, there you go. To this exciting life you have. You have done so much, and now you have more you will do. I so envy you. I am looking to study here in Wien. Music. I love music, and this is the soul of music. The classic, I mean. Even the waltz. In this city of dreams, as they call it."

She let out a long, protracted sigh as she looked at me square in the eyes.

"Dreams, Hunter. Did you know they call Wien the city of dreams?"

I shook my head.

"They do. And do you know why? Because of a Jew. A Jew named Sigmund Freud. You know of this man, of course. This great thinker. And now suddenly I do not want to study music anymore. I want to see the world. Like you. You make everything seem so easy and exciting. Like *poof*. You just go and do things."

"Do you have a scholarship or something?" I asked her. "I don't know much about Poland, but how can you just leave it? I thought everything was so closed there. So strict. And money. It's so expensive here. How can you afford to live here, much less study here?"

She looked at me as if pondering my question and how to answer it.

"How can I afford it?" she mused. "Yes, of course, how can it be such a closed society, a worker's paradise, and someone gets to come to the great Wien and study music? I must tell you something first, Hunter. I can afford it if I live cheaply. Like in this hostel, even though I have my own room. I want to be honest with you. You are so honest with me. So free with me about your life.

"How can I afford it? My father owns—maybe that is not the word. The state owns everything. My father is the chief of the largest construction company in Poland. I am not of the proletariat, Hunter. And that is all nonsense about the proletariat. It is so complicated in my country.

"What did it say in the story *1984*? No, not *1984*.

But in the story *Animal Farm*. This novel about my country. Or like my country, not Poland itself, I think. Both stories written by George Orwell. I am not supposed to read such propaganda against the great worker's paradise that my country is. Or is supposed to be. But when I leave to come to places like Wien, that's exactly what I read. What did it say in this novel called *Animal Farm*? Everyone is equal."

"Except that," I interrupted her with a sly grin, "some are more equal than others."

"Completely this, Hunter. I love my country, Hunter. And I love my father. But I am Polish. But not my father's Poland. Not Russian puppet Poland. I grew up atheist. But no one is really atheist in the Soviet Bloc because the state is god. But inside of me now I am Catholic and free. Free inside. I am not so religious Catholic. I am political Catholic.

"And also like you explained about being a Jew last night. How you do not must be religious to be of this group, this tribe as you called it last night. The tribe of Jew. I am like from tribe of Catholic. Even if I am not fully religious. Poland is Catholic, and this is my tribe. It is like this karma I hear about. How in Poland we tormented the Jews and now it is we Catholics that are treated so. I am Catholic Polish now, not Russian Polish.

"I am grateful for the privileges from my father's position. But Hunter, I am a free woman. Polish and free. And I love our new Polish pope, John Paul II. I am so proud to be Polish and free."

She looked piercingly at me, determined and confident, the last of her shyness gone.

"I do not have to study immediately, Hunter. Now I

want to wait to study. I must arrange things first. For my new dreams. It will be difficult, but I can do it. I have friends at our embassy. Perhaps they tell my father, but I can talk to him. Here is what I want to say to you now. Can you stay in Wien until I get my visas? I can arrange visas to these countries where you are going. I have a special passport. Like diplomat. Special favor for me, the more equal Polish. Can you take me with you? Does this idea shock you?"

I didn't answer but let my concern show.

"I want to go with you, Hunter. I will be a good companion to you. I like that you are big and experienced and an American Marine. I feel safe with you in these dangerous places for me. With you and my special connections, I will be a good companion to you if you take me with you. Is that all right with you? Will you do that for me?"

Slowly, a smile spread on my face. This was the greatest idea alive, so I nodded.

"Yes, Ewa, I would love for you to go with me. I don't have much money and will have to travel cheap and don't want to live off of you. We will have to take crowded buses and trains and sleep in bad hostels in poor countries. You can take a couple of dresses with you, but you need more durable clothes. Blue jeans and flannel."

"That's what I want. To wear rough clothes and to travel like a real person. I have friends I can leave my other belongings with, here in Wien. But I have money. I hope you do not mind. I will not spend it. I will live cheap like you do. But I have money. I do not just want to see the world. I want to live the world. With you, Hunter. With someone like you."

Chapter 3

I planned on entering Turkey from Greece. That way I only needed visas for my Asian countries, beginning with Turkey. I still had to pass through a Communist country to get there, Yugoslavia, but it was the one European Communist country that was not in the Soviet sphere. It was even considered pro-West. And it only required my passport to enter, no visa. I wasn't sure if Ewa had to get a visa for it, and I didn't ask. I felt she needed to handle things her *special* way, and I felt uncomfortable with intruding in her affairs.

Ewa preferred we pass through Bulgaria instead of Greece, however. That meant I had to get an additional visa. Since I had to wait for Ewa to get her visas anyway, it was little inconvenience for me to do so. Bulgaria was more direct than Greece in getting to the Bosporus Strait, so that was a plus in going through the country. But mostly, she wanted me to see an Eastern Bloc country first hand, which Bulgaria was.

Austria was breathtakingly beautiful as we began our travel by bus through it to Yugoslavia. It had rivers, hills, and mountains all along the way.

And cold. I hated the cold. I struggled with the cold. Being from southern Texas, I never acclimated to such brutal weather as I faced in northern Europe.

Yugoslavia was also cold, but at least farther south, giving me hope for relief soon. The scenery in

Yugoslavia couldn't match that of Austria, but it still had much natural beauty of its own, with its hills, forests, and mountains.

Life, however, appeared dismal there to me. The smog was the worst I had ever seen, and it seemed at least twenty years behind northern Europe in its economy. The cars were old, as were the buildings and streets, as well as the buses we rode. People did not seem happy there, only surviving. I took it to be an example of socialism at its worst, but I also knew it was a country of many nationalities and ethnic groups. Perhaps this too presented problems in getting things to function smoothly there. I could only speculate.

There was also anxiety over Yugoslavia's future as a nation, that once its revered leader, Tito, died, it would not last as a country but would divide into several small countries. That concern also may well have put a damper on life and economy in Yugoslavia.

"Look," Ewa said casually while pointing to the jagged mountains we rode past on the narrow highway. "These are unique structures. I read about them. These mountains are made out of a special granite."

The mountains led us to a narrow rapids. Below our highway, a small raft bounced from one current to another while trying to survive small dips that occurred. Somehow the guy shooting these rapids on the raft was managing a long wooden pole, which he used to guide his craft. It reminded me in part of a rodeo, the way he held on for dear life whenever the raft jerked on a boulder in the river. Ewa smiled brightly as she looked at the raft, then at me to share the scene, then back again at the raft.

I enjoyed knowing I was in a Communist country,

and I enjoyed the scenery, but it was a depressing place to me, overall. The one good aspect was when we switched over to a train in Belgrade. The train was yet another old and dingy box to sit in, but one where we somehow managed to have a compartment for ourselves. Soon it would be night, and Ewa spread out her sleeping bag on one full-length seat, while I took the one across from her.

As the twilight settled in behind the mountains, we felt the quiet it seemed to create, a lonely quiet that wanted relief. I could see only her silhouette as we sat upright across from each other by the window. The dim light allowed us to look at one another now, as if not intruding.

"What is your favorite time so far on the trip, Hunter?"

"The Alps," I emphasized.

"You mean in Austria?"

"Yes. I just love the mountains. Where I grew up in Texas was near the ocean and very flat. I love the ocean even more than the mountains, but I do so love mountains, and the Alps are glorious. They seem so proud."

"I agree," she said with a sigh. "They are so majestic. It is so green in Austria, and the lakes in the Alps are an added treat. But you know, strange as it sounds, I loved it when we came upon the man on the raft with the bagpipe. You know, earlier this afternoon here in Yugoslavia. Just before we got on the train in Belgrade. After we saw the rapids, just after that, where a man was like celebrating being finished with the danger and excitement of the rapids and playing with joy on his bagpipes."

"Is that what they were?" I asked. "They sounded like bagpipes and resembled them a bit. It did have a bag of some sort, and tubes and pipes."

"He was so much in a good mood," she continued. "I enjoyed his music and also his spirit. His feeling of triumph. The bag comes from a cow's stomach. Maybe it is a goat's stomach. No, no, I'm sure a pig's stomach, actually. My goodness, I cannot remember. How is that? I have seen this instrument before, but cannot remember from which animal I was told. I love the human spirit, Hunter. How even in the remote and poor and depressed Yugoslavian countryside there is this spirit to invent their own bagpipe. And to live in triumph of defeating the rapids. What joy."

"I'm glad you shared this with me, Ewa. I was sort of down on Yugoslavia. It is pretty. Nothing like Austria, but it does have a natural beauty. I want to appreciate it, but the country seems so drab to me. And dirty. I saw little of the human spirit here. But then in the most trivial scene you found your biggest joy. I love that. I'm glad you're here with me."

Even in the faint glow, I saw a smile come onto her face as I spoke those words. I wanted to say them again because I liked making her happy. She was worthy of happiness.

"I am tired now, Hunter. We have travelled hard since Wien, and now we can have a good night's sleep. By morning we will be in Bulgaria."

Only the rumble of the train could be heard. It induced sleep as much as how tired we were. I could feel myself drifting almost as soon as I lay inside my sleeping bag.

"Are you asleep?" I soon heard Ewa ask.

"Almost."

"I just wanted to tell you how happy I am with you," Ewa said in a sweet, vulnerable voice. "I would have never done this if I had not met you. You are a good companion."

As simple as her words were, they touched me. I didn't want to sleep now. I wanted to be with her, not just lie across the aisle from her in silence. I wanted to be next to her. I wanted to hear her heart beating.

"Good night, Hunter," she said just above a whisper.

"Good night, Ewa. Sleep well."

Chapter 4

Everything changed on our arrival at the Bulgarian border. Customs people are not the friendliest people to begin with, but the guards we encountered treated us with disdain, as if we were a nuisance, or worse. When I showed my American passport, I was given the onceover as their stern glares toward me bounced from my passport, and the visa in it, to me personally. Was I an enemy of the people or someone to be moved along like cattle? Or vermin?

When they saw Ewa's passport, a look of surprise came over their faces. Was it a shock to see a Polish girl come over in a train from Yugoslavia instead of Romania, or was it because she was with an American?

Such treatment didn't occur only at the border, either. Our bus stopped to let police inspectors check everyone's papers at each town and village. It took over an hour to reach Sofia, the nation's capital, a mere fifty miles away.

This probably explains why I noticed little of the countryside. We were always being stopped, and it got me in a defensive, disgruntled mood. When I looked outside, it was foggy and dreary. Somehow typical, I decided. I saw some open fields, a few forests and hills, but so much looked bleak to me. The expressionless people on the bus just added to my mood.

As we entered Sofia, we were greeted by a large

statue of Lenin, tall, erect, and commanding, the epitome of a great leader, just like in pictures I had seen of such statues in the Soviet Union. I glanced over at Ewa, sitting next to me. Like the other passengers, her expression was blank and empty.

"What do we do now?" I asked her after we disembarked. "Have you anything in mind?"

"We should find a hotel," she suggested.

Until now, we had ridden the buses and trains straight through, even sleeping on them. The thought of a hotel was appealing, but I was going to let her do the talking. I was thinking she knew her way around better, but I also wanted her to feel in charge and to trust me.

Ewa talked to the lady at a check-in desk. Some Slavic language, I was sure, but I had no idea if it was Bulgarian. The clerk handed Ewa back our passports as well as our keys. I wasn't really sure if we shared the same room, but as soon as I turned to go upstairs, the clerk looked at me, smiled mischievously, and winked. What the hell did that mean? But it was my first clue that Ewa and I would be sharing our lodging.

In our room there was a small desk against the middle of the back wall. A yard from that and next to the outside wall was a small dresser with three drawers for our clothes. The room had two single beds, with a yard of space between and not much more than that between the beds and each of the side walls. I was worried if the length of the bed was enough for my Texas-sized body. Since the bed had a headboard and footboard, if I was too tall, I was stuck, since the bed was too narrow for me to sleep at an angle.

Our room had a window that did not open. Under the windowsill was an oil-fueled heater. Ewa didn't say a word but chose the bed nearest the window. She threw her backpack onto it and silently began to unpack.

"I need to hand wash my clothes," she said, barely looking up from unpacking. "There is no sink here. I must take my douche—how do you say, my bath—and use my soap also for my clothes. I did not bring many clothes exchanges. I brought one nice dress and dress shoes, and only two rough sets of clothes besides what I am wearing. So I must wash every day while we stay in Sofia."

While we stay in Sofia. What did that mean? It seemed a drab city. I had no desire to stay. Just a good wash and sleep, a Bulgarian meal, and on to Turkey, as far as I was concerned. But it was my first Eastern Bloc country. She was Polish. Why not?

"Are you hungry?" I asked her.

"Not so much," she said with a polite smile. "Where we ate when we changed buses at the border left me satisfied. Are you still hungry, Hunter?"

I held back a smirk. So the snack we had back at the border had satisfied her, had it?

"While you're bathing and washing your clothes," I said, "I'll look around. Just to get a feel. And get a sandwich or something."

"You wish not to go somewhere with me?" she asked. "I speak the language. Not so well, but it is Slavic, and I can understand with effort."

"Yes, I can wait to go out with you. I even hoped you'd explain things to me along the way. But let me stretch my legs and grab a sandwich, and then I'll come back and wash up."

I walked down the three flights of stairs from our

room to the check-in at the entrance of the hotel, then out into the street. There was a park nearby, and I followed the sidewalk to the side of it. Surely there would be some tourist-type shops around.

Just in front of the park was the bus station where we'd arrived. This had kiosks, I remembered. And there was a tourist information office just inside it. Perfect.

"What is there to do in Sofia?" I asked a man behind the desk near the entrance of the tourist information. With him was a woman and another man. They were playing a card game. All three looked up at me curiously. I waited for an answer to my question, but the blank stares from them continued. "I am a tourist," I added.

"What want you to do?" The man nearest to me asked. He wore a disgruntled look.

"I'm not sure," I replied. "I just got here and don't know anything about Sofia."

"Eat you?" The other man asked me, still showing consternation on his face.

The other two went back to playing cards.

"Yes, please. But I'll get that at a kiosk. What kind of activities do you have for tourists?"

"Activities?" He asked this with a harsh accent. It seemed to cause him pain.

Maybe Ewa could get better results, I decided. I smiled and walked back out.

There was a grill inside the train station. I pointed at a bratwurst to the woman behind the counter, paid my Bulgarian *lev*, their currency, and began nibbling as I walked back to the hotel. The bratwurst was good. In my mood, I was almost surprised.

By the time I got back to our room, Ewa had

returned from the bathroom. She wore a fresh change of blue jeans with a dark green sweatshirt, making her look like a college girl back home. The clothes she'd washed, including underwear, lay dripping on the wall heater, getting dry. It made for a cozy domestic scene.

"Hallo, Hunter." She smiled as I walked to my bed to retrieve my backpack. "Did you get something to eat? Do you wish to bathe and wash your clothes now before we stroll the sidewalks outside? The WC—no, not that word. How do you call this in English? Bathroom?" She looked at me for approval of her choice of words. I nodded. "The bathroom is small. And the only one on this floor. A toilet, a mirror over a sink, and a bathtub. I hope you did not want to take a shower. There is only a bath. I prefer a shower, but a bath is fine also. If you need soap, I have some for you. There is no soap or towel in the WC. Is that all right with you?"

"I have soap and a towel. Thanks."

"Good. I will finish laying out my clothes. The room is cheap, Hunter. I hope you do not mind, but I paid already for two nights. I should have asked you. The money I gave her as we came in the hotel to check in, that was for two nights. You do not owe me. Please. I want to show you around. I do not know the city, but it is my chance to show you a Soviet country. Or at least a city in one. We must still travel through most of Bulgaria to reach Turkey. But while we are here, let me show you Sofia and explain about life under the Soviets. Is that good with you? I should have asked how long you want to stay. I will not take advantage to impose my way again. But please, allow me this time. Is that good with you?"

I nodded an acceptance of her plan. I wasn't in a hurry anyway. Two days in Sofia, Bulgaria, with a Polish girl. I liked the idea now that the reality was upon me.

"There's a tourist information near the train station," I commented. "I didn't get anywhere with them, though. It was like I disrupted their vacation. Maybe if you talk to them it will go better."

"What do you need to know, Hunter? There are mountains here. We have no car for travel, but we can see mountains from here in the city. The Vitosha Mountain is the big one here. There are no rivers, I think. It is the city, the people in it, I want to show you. But we can go to this information place."

"Finish up with your unpacking, Ewa. I'll be quick with my bath. I won't wash my clothes today, since we'll be here tomorrow. I'll wash then."

Once on the street, the first thing we did was head back to the tourist information office. The same three agents were there as I'd encountered earlier. Looks of concern appeared when they recognized me. Soon, Ewa was chattering away with them.

It was the same show even with her, however. One talked with her while the other two continued their card game. Ewa started off in her calm, sweet voice, but by the end of the conversation she became more intense. Finally, she walked away.

"It was not good with them, Hunter," she explained. "I asked about restaurants, about tourist sites, even about hotels. They knew nothing. Not exactly nothing. They mentioned that there were some restaurants around, even museums, but they could not tell me one. Just somewhere out there. It was enough for me to know they existed somehow. The man that talked with me so much seemed to wonder why I wanted to know."

"It looked more like he wondered why you were bothering him."

"Yes," she concurred, showing frustration. "I interrupted their card game, I think. It is much this way in Warsaw and other cities. This is what I want you to see, this situation. I am sorry, Hunter, and embarrassed, but actually, it is funny, no? Disgusting, but funny."

"So what do you want to do for the rest of the day, Ewa?"

"While we are near the tourist places, we can seek out a restaurant for later when we are hungry for dinner. And just walk around to see what else is in the tourist part of the city. But tomorrow let us go to the more mundane areas, where the local people live."

I was not impressed with Sofia, even the supposed tourist area. Sofia seemed plain and blasé at best, stripped, and dismal. The people never smiled, nor were they in any kind of hurry. The sky was continually cloudy, which was seasonal weather, but it fit the gloom of the city.

"What do you like to eat, Hunter?" Ewa asked me after a couple of hours walking and window shopping.

"Food," I said jokingly. "I don't care. What is typical cuisine? Do you know?"

"While we are here, let us eat what is common. You noticed I read occasionally a book while we were travelling. It was a travel book, and it had a chapter about Bulgaria. So we will find a tourist restaurant, so no need for ration tickets. There are stews with pork, goat, lamb, veal, chicken, or beef. This is the same for soups. In the stew and the soup are also vegetables."

"I shouldn't eat pork."

"I understand, Hunter. Do you like sausage? But many times there is pork in sausage."

"I already had one. Let's try something different."

"They serve food from Greece and also the Middle East."

"That sounds great. I love Greek food. And I lived in Israel, so I also love Middle Eastern food. But I'll try local while we're here. Unless we can't stand it, and then we'll try Greek."

"Good. We will walk more, and I will read from the menu at the door of the restaurant."

There were several food stands around, and also indoor restaurants. Back home we would call them "greasy spoons." Ewa patiently read from the menus, or if they didn't have one, she looked inside to see what customers were having.

"This one has many Bulgarian dishes," she said, looking at me inquisitively. "Do you like yogurt?"

"Yes, but I'd prefer meat for supper."

"How does this sound to you? There is a lamb soup, but it has many sour vegetables and herbs. Pickles, things like that."

I shook my head no.

"They have vegetable soups."

I shook my head again.

"Soup made with fish?" she asked.

Again I shook my head no.

"There is so much pork on the menu, even with the grilled meats—pork, pork, and more pork. Is chicken all right for you? Are you in the mood? Or grilled fish?"

"Chicken is fine," I replied.

"Grilled tongue?" she threw in even after I agreed to chicken.

"Chicken," I answered almost desperately. "Chicken is fine."

"May I eat pork?" she asked me politely. "Is that a problem for you?"

"I'm okay if you eat pork."

"Good, we can go inside. They also have goat cheese. I will take some of that also."

I wanted a salad to go with my chicken, so at Ewa's suggestion I ordered something called *shopska*, which included chopped cucumbers, onions, peppers, tomatoes, and feta cheese. It was wonderful. I was satisfied that I'd enjoyed something in Bulgaria, finally. I hadn't really enjoyed many things since I left Austria and was wondering if I was too harsh or demanding.

Ewa and I were tired. It was enough for one day. We made our way back to the hotel just past dark. Hopefully a long and good sleep would renew us. It had been a long two days to get from Vienna to Sofia.

"I must turn out the light, Hunter. Then we can change into sleeping clothes. I have only a cotton shirt in which to sleep, and my underwear. Good night. I had a wonderful day with you."

In my time in Western Bloc countries of northern Europe, as well as in Israel, girls were not shy. Common courtesy, as well as not wanting to encourage aggressive behavior from a guy, meant a girl might be prudent about how much of her body she exposed, but she certainly wasn't ashamed to expose anything if it came down to it. So I still didn't know about Ewa and her familiarity with men. Was she just being cautious, polite, or shy, or was she strict about any suggestiveness at all?

Even with the light off, glimmers behind the drawn curtains from the window exposed our silhouettes. I didn't want to be rude, or get caught, but I glanced at her disrobing from the corner of my eyes, as I also disrobed. She neatly folded her clothes at the foot of her bed, so I did the same with mine. My gaze followed her form as she made her way under the cover.

Men are pathetic creatures, I laughed to myself while rolling over to my side to go to sleep. The rush I got from just this little tease blew my mind.

"Hunter," Ewa said, just above a whisper.

"You okay?" I asked while I turned my head toward her slightly.

"I am sorry, but do you mind to turn back around to me? At least until I go to sleep. It is worse than being alone to know you are facing the other way."

The vulnerability and sweetness in her voice was the most seductive feeling I'd had in months, if not years. Was I going to survive my time with Ewa?

I rolled over to my other side, facing her.

"I had a wonderful time with you today, Ewa. You really travel well. I enjoyed it."

I watched her extend an arm toward me.

"Can we touch, then?" she asked me sweetly.

I reached out to gently hold her hand, as if this was a form of goodnight kiss. I felt tears of affection welling up inside me as I did so. I was a lost cause. India seemed like a hopelessly long journey away; would I be able to survive emotions already beginning?

The next morning, to be polite, I grabbed my clothes from the headboard of my bed and put them on while she was still asleep. When I saw her begin to wake up, I said, "I'm just going to the bathroom," as I got up to leave.

"Did you sleep well?" she asked with a happy smile.

"I don't know if I'm caught up, but it sure helped."

"It was very nice sleep," she said with a chirp in her voice. "We have another night in this hotel. Maybe tomorrow we are ready to continue on to Istanbul."

There were government stores outside the tourist area. Papers and ration coupons were required for these stores. As we inspected them from the outside, Ewa began to explain things, as if on a mission.

"Do you see the lines? How can you be productive for the economy and wait so long in line for so few things? Or have a life? People shop and then present their allotments. Not just money, but you are not allowed to have more than a fair share." She looked at me for emphasis. "I think this government, this Russian puppet government, loves control. It is as much about control as it is about shortages of goods, or for fairness. They have power. Much power, but never enough meat, bread, or cereals. Or clothing. Or housing. We live in houses not so much bigger than our hotel room."

"If they want more food, why can't they go to the tourist areas?"

"It is too expensive there for the proletariat. And those are a way to make money from the foreign barbarians. Charge them more in the tourist areas to subsidize the masses. Except there are so few tourists."

She returned her stare to the store in front of us.

"My father provided for me," she continued, "since we were more equal than the others. I am not angry with my father for getting more. I am angry at the great genius Lenin, who decided we must live this way as you see in the store. I do not tell my father what I do when I leave Poland. I do not want to lose my privileges. But when I first saw West Berlin, I could not imagine there was such a world. A world of choices and wealth, even for the proletariat. And no lines, no shortages, not like in the Soviet Union, anyway. Ever since I first saw West Berlin as a little girl, I wanted to see more of this world I am denied. When I first saw Wien, I began to read and to talk to people. And now I know that when the czar ruled Russia, Russia was the world's largest exporter of wheat. Yes, he was a tyrant, but not as much as our great comrade Lenin. And there are shortages now. Why? Because of overpopulation? Because of no land or money or seeds? It is because of Lenin and Stalin and everyone since. The system cannot provide. We are supposed to need this government to even survive. We must survive their system and their shortages from this insane bullying system."

She looked up at me with an apologetic smile, then put her arm inside of mine.

"Let us go, Hunter. I wanted to show you this."

As Ewa and I returned to the tourist area, I thought back to my time in the Marines and how we were told by the "new age" that we were all brainwashed into believing bad things about Communism. And in many ways we were. The young must be taught. There are rules and ideals. There is right versus wrong. When I first heard the war challenged in the sixties, it made an impression on me. It didn't make me want to burn the flag or feel bitter, but it made me want to know more about the complexity of everything. When I heard arguments against the war, or wealth, or racism, or other aspects I took for granted, I thought about them. There was a side to some of these arguments that I was shocked to find out. When I read about early American socialists like Eugene Debs and Norman Thomas, I wondered why people hated them. They weren't totalitarian. I didn't think socialism worked as well as they seemed to think, and definitely not as well as capitalism, but I followed some of the thinking.

Life was indeed complex, except that much of my generation seemed to think traditional America was simply wrong, if not evil. There was indeed evil in America that we needed to come to grips with. I couldn't deny that. But that is a learning and maturing process, in fact. However, there were virtues about America, too, just as I had been taught. And even with the evil about us, why did our evil make the Communists not evil? Why was everything suddenly so simplistic again, just with different values?

Somehow Ewa and I, from our vastly different upbringings, independently ended up on the same page. The challenge of life had gotten us here, I concluded, and the way we wanted to know things. And that was the beauty of it all—how we wanted to understand things.

We went back to the hotel shortly after eating. We had washing to do. But also, it was our last chance to feel at home with one another before being stuck on trains and buses again.

"Hunter, hold my hand now," Ewa said boldly that night before we drifted off to sleep. "Let us celebrate such a wonderful day together."

"You are a great companion, Ewa. I can't imagine going to India without you."

With that, Ewa pushed off her bedcover to crawl into bed next to me.

"I will sleep with you tonight, Hunter. I am nervous about any sexual things, so be patient with me. But I want to be next to you all night. For the warmth and the comfort."

I put my arms around her and held her head next to mine.

"I am ready to fall out of the bed, though, Hunter. Let us push the beds together."

We got up to do so, then placed a folded blanket over the crack at the joining of the two beds, for comfort. I never wanted to sleep without her again.

Chapter 5

Entering Turkey was exciting in that it was yet another country I had never seen before. Even better, Turkey was special in history. And I loved history. From the Bible there was Ephesus, Smyrna, Attalia, and Mount Ararat, not to mention the Hittites. Then in later history was the Ottoman Empire. Modern Turkey is in NATO. And though now a secular democracy, Turkey was my first Muslim country.

Soon we reached the Bosporus Strait, by which lay Istanbul, formerly known as Constantinople. Long after Rome fell, Constantinople ruled the mightiest part of the Roman Empire, known as Byzantium. It became the epitome of glory and grandeur. And now as part of Turkey, Istanbul still held a mystique.

Ancient Constantinople was the largest and richest urban center in the Eastern Mediterranean in its day. This was a result of its strategic position in the trade routes between the Aegean and Black Seas. At its peak, it was the richest and largest European city, dominating cultural and economic life. Beautiful monasteries and churches, in particular Hagia Sophia, or the Church of Holy Wisdom, graced the city.

Constantinople preserved manuscripts of Greek and Latin authors throughout a period when instability and disorder caused their mass destruction in Western Europe and northern Africa after the fall of Rome.

These same documents were later brought by refugees to Italy, where they played a key part in stimulating the Renaissance and creating a transition to the modern world. Constantinople was without parallel anywhere in Europe for a thousand years.

Even the smog and horrendous traffic of the modern Istanbul that greeted Ewa and me upon our arrival didn't dampen my excitement. Just knowing I was in this marvelous city let me come to terms with these blemishes, whereas in Yugoslavia and Bulgaria, I was disgusted by such.

Once Ewa and I got out of the bus station, we looked for a hotel. Common sense told us that any hotel near the station would be overpriced, but we were on foot and didn't know our way around. Nor were we in the mood to scramble for a place. We were tired and wanted to dump our gear.

When we found a hotel several blocks away that had the same price as one comparable a block before, we took it. That was our cue we were past the worst tourist rip-off places.

Even our small hotel room in Sofia was better than what we settled for our first night in Istanbul. It was just as small, but also old. Everything about it was old. The structure, the furniture, the beddings, and desk. There not only was no bathroom in our room, there weren't any windows either. The room was dingy, with smudges and stains. Even worse was how the one bathroom on our floor was next to us, and it stank, enough so that we could smell it in our room.

"Did you pay for two nights?" Ewa asked me desperately.

"Just for tonight," I assured her. "We'll find a

better room tomorrow. It means we'll have to take our backpacks with us and start again before we can do any real sightseeing."

"And we will inspect the room," she insisted. "I will not wash my clothes tonight or bathe. We will go out to eat, then only sleep here, then leave the first thing in the morning."

I nodded agreement.

It made our stroll through the streets of Istanbul all the more important that afternoon as we looked for a restaurant. It allowed us to stay away from our depressing hotel room.

There was an appeal to Istanbul later that night, however, that let us forget the misery of our room entirely. The entire city was lit up and bustling, exuding energy—perhaps too much energy. We couldn't cross the streets successfully. If there were traffic lights, they were ignored by the onslaught of cars. Endless streams of cars barged along willy-nilly, on a first-come-first-served basis, and we had to dodge and weave at each intersection in order to cross.

"Do you see a place you would like to eat?" Ewa asked me.

"They all look good. Nothing fancy yet, which we can't afford anyway. Happy people are gorging themselves. I lived in Israel, and they were part of the Ottoman Empire for centuries, as Palestine, of course. So Israel had Middle Eastern but also Turkish dishes. And Turkish coffee."

"So, Hunter, what you are telling me is that there is something in mind that you would like to have tonight."

"Yes, I'd love some *swarma*. God, that is good stuff—shaved lamb and beef over a grill, in flat bread, with vegetables. So I know I like that. We can go inside a place and look. We'll see what others are eating, and if we aren't happy, we can always eat swarma or falafel."

The restaurants reminded me of Mexico with their relaxed and friendly atmospheres, and we soon settled in one.

"Oh, yes, Hunter!" Ewa swooned as we ate. "Swarma is marvelous. Oh, we will never go hungry while we are in Turkey. I just hope I will not get fat. The cucumbers and tomatoes are of the gods, I think. They are wonderful. I do not care for this coffee, though. What is the big marvel over sipping through coffee grinds floating on the top?"

"Tomorrow," I instructed, "after we find a hotel, I want to go to the mosques around Hagia Sophia. Right on the Bosporus Strait."

"You are in charge, my Hunter man," she replied with a grin.

Once we returned to our room, however, with its dinginess and pungent odor, our moods dampened again.

It was pitch black as I turned off the light, except for the tiniest glimmer of hallway light from under the door. Ewa and I immediately embraced and for the first time shared an affectionate goodnight kiss. I could feel the bed springs inside the thin mattress under the sheet as I did so.

Before eating breakfast the next morning, we found a hotel near us that was much nicer. It was twice as expensive but still cheap. We even had our own bathroom attached to our bedroom. And the bed was firm, new, and clean.

After unpacking, we began our walk through Istanbul for sightseeing. We had no bearing or reference except for the Bosporus Strait itself. Then we saw it—the Hagia Sophia mosque.

"It is so beautiful," Ewa sighed as we gasped at the structure from a distance.

"So proud and majestic," I added in awe.

"It was a church once," Ewa commented. "The Muslims conquered so many places, and somehow everything sacred from before was now their personal sacredness."

"But Ewa, the Christians under Constantine didn't build Hagia Sophia either. They enhanced it as a church, for sure. But before Constantine came along it was a pagan temple."

"So I cannot complain then, you are telling me."

"Yes, you can, Ewa. I understand. But the truth is that all cultures and conquerors have a knack for converting sacred places and things into their own. It's human nature. After the Ottoman Empire died at the end of World War I, secularism seemed sacred to the new Turkey, you might say. The new ruler, Ataturk, was a secular guy. To him, Turkey had decayed as it got more and more stuck in religious doctrine that dictated the Ottoman Empire. So under his rule he not only secularized Turkey but also this mosque. The minarets are still here, but inside, the building itself is a museum now."

"Each new religion has a new temple," Ewa replied as she followed my logic. "Even the secular god makes demands, it seems."

"We might enjoy the museum," I said, as we began walking towards it. "Plus, right next to it is the Blue

Mosque. It's still a mosque. I'd like to see it also."

Muslim architecture fascinated me, especially its mosques—the domes, minarets, and arches, the vast open interiors and courtyards, the art inside, including verses from the Qu'ran around the periphery written in Arabic. Even the Arabic script looked poetic somehow.

As much as Ewa and I were enthralled by this historic city, its size made it difficult to get around. So we let the Hagia Sophia area and our stroll along the Bosporus be enough for us.

Though Turkey was a secular, democratic country, Ewa and I made a point of not showing public displays of affection or even holding hands. Even in Sofia we got glares and admonishments when Ewa placed her arm inside of mine once as we walked. The history and scenes of Istanbul put us in a romantic mode to where we occasionally held hands to share the moment, but we quickly returned to being casual tourists.

Our spirits were upbeat when we returned to our room just before dusk. I let Ewa use the bath first, and with our newfound freedom of having our own private bathroom, she took the liberty of wearing only a towel wrapped around her as she walked to her bed after her bath, much like Brigitte Bardot who was so famous in my youth.

When I returned with my washed clothes, Ewa was reading, and still wearing only her towel. My heart skipped. As I hung my clothes, she put back the bed covers, took off her towel, and lay down waiting for me.

"Please, likewise," she stated bluntly about my nightclothes as she patted my part of the bed next to her.

I obliged before getting into bed next to her.

"I am a virgin," she whispered as she caressed my neck. "Be patient with me. I am very nervous, but I want to be with you so boldly. I do not think I can go the depth of the physical tonight, but to be bold now helps my courage. I want you to be the one to make me a woman. A complete woman, I mean. But tonight let us just linger naturally. No sex yet, if you do not mind."

I stroked her forehead tenderly with my fingertips as I lay snugly against her. I could feel her breasts on me. Trust and desire exuded from her.

Chapter 6

The only thing I remember of significance about Ankara, Turkey's capital, was how I read in an international American newspaper while there about an American religious cult committing mass suicide in the jungles of Guyana in South America, taking with them to eternity a US congressman from California who had been there investigating their situation.

Ankara itself seemed like just another Turkish city, a bigger and more crowded one that seemed not to have any distinct personality. Even the night Ewa and I spent in Ankara was uneventful, at least concerning the anticipation we had, going into it, about ourselves. Each night spent in a hotel until then had brought out more feelings of desire in us. But without saying a word, Ewa crawled into bed in her undergarments and went straight to sleep during our one night in Ankara. We barely even kissed. I had to assume it was cold feet on her part, but it may have been Ankara itself.

The terrain was arid going through Turkey and became steadily more so the closer we got to Iran. The mountains were snow capped in parts, but mostly there was little vegetation. What I liked about travelling in Turkey, however, was how music played over the speakers in the bus. I loved the intoxicating rhythms from this music. African strains are famous for their sharp, terse rhythms, and rightly so, but these

Turkish—perhaps even Arabic—rhythms were just as penetrating, with an elongated hierarchy of pronounced beats intermingling with weaker ones.

Turkey itself, on the highway from Istanbul to Erzurum near the Iranian border, had vast, open spaces, with just enough mountains interspersed to thwart any monotony that may have formed. The people were often gruff. It was a hardy life in these places, with hardy people. Some places were so poor, in fact, and with so few tourists, it proved difficult to find enjoyable food. In one village where we stopped for breakfast, all I managed was Turkish flat bread with a slice of butter. The butter was hard and wouldn't spread. To eat it, I imitated the locals by taking a bite from the bread, then a bite into the butter separately while I chewed.

I was nervous as we crossed into Iran. I'd heard nothing but bad things about it in recent years. The Shah and his American allies were very unpopular. Speculation had the Shah on the verge of being overthrown. Americans were warned not to go there. But here I was. And with Ewa.

Iran was even drier than Turkey. How could that be? I had pictured Iran to be that way from descriptions and pictures, but I never understood how ancient Persia could have been one of the world's great historic empires looking like it did. Hardy places produce hardy people, I got that. The Persian conqueror Cyrus the Great made a point of that, in fact. But somewhere you had to be able to produce—goods, things, assets. Yet Iran was bleak. It had oil, but I wasn't sure what else. Somehow, however, the despised Americans were modernizing the economy.

"Do not go to Tehran," the border guard told Ewa

and me as we left Turkey going into Iran. "They hate Americans."

I nodded an acknowledgment his way as we reboarded our bus.

"The Shah is hated," an agent at the currency exchange just inside Iran told us. "Beware. The Shah is America's puppet. There is danger for Americans in Tehran. Do not go there."

These threats concerned me, for sure, but I was a rural Texan and a Marine on top of that, so these warnings also challenged me. In my eyes, I wasn't looking for trouble; I just wanted to see the world and go overland to India. Still, I hated the thought of backing away from trouble. It was this attitude, as much as believing in the Vietnam War itself, that had induced me to join the Marines to begin with. My generation's animosity about the military also brought this defiance out in me. Someone always telling me what to do induced a belligerent attitude inside me.

Then what about Ewa? I cared for her and felt responsible for her. What was I dragging her into? I had to be cautious then in spite of myself.

"We are all night on the bus," she whispered from the seat next to me. "We are still so far from Tehran. And we are the only Europeans on this bus. Everyone stares at us. I cannot go to sleep, but I cannot stay awake either."

"Put your head on my shoulder. That'll help you sleep."

"Do you see how the men look at me? I am afraid to even touch you. What do they think of me? Am I a prostitute?"

"The more religious ones, I have a feeling, think

you should be riding at the back of the bus. By yourself."

"But this is not a *sharia* country. Why can I not ride next to my husband?"

I looked at her, charmed by what she said.

"Where there is sharia," I commented, "even riding with your husband isn't allowed. I've heard that, anyway. And for the religious ones, they already hate the Shah and how sharia is not allowed here. All the more they resent you, I think."

"How many are so religious on this bus do you suppose, Hunter?"

"I don't know. Did you hear that guy playing the tape to the mullah behind us? I guess he's a mullah anyway, with his turban. Don't look back. He's just a couple of seats behind us. They talked forever, and I can guess what about. Then he played that tape."

"The one with the crying?"

"Yes. The tape was from the Qu'ran, I think. Later, while you were napping, a man across the aisle told me about the tape before he got off. He said an imam was reading from the Qu'ran on it, and the message was so deep and eventful he wailed as he read. Then this mullah guy from behind us looked at me. I mean right at me. You weren't touching me or anything, just lying back in your seat asleep for a while. He smiled, but it wasn't a friendly smile. It wasn't malicious or anything, but like checking me out."

"Why did we come to this dreadful place, Hunter? Let us not stay. Please. I beg you."

"It's a big country, Ewa. It will take us three days just to pass straight through. We won't dwell in any one spot, but let's pick our spots to stay along the way."

I heard her sigh.

"It'll be okay," I lied. "The Shah is still in power, and there are other Americans here. Nothing happens to them. Iran is modernizing. We won't hang around long, but there are some things I want to see. The rumor is the Shah is ready to abdicate. I want to check out attitudes and find out more about it. I know there are fanatics here, but most are normal people."

"I need to tell you something, Hunter. Please do not feel anger at me."

I looked at her curiously.

"While we were in Wien getting our visas, I got a marriage certificate for us. You have an American passport and I have a Polish one, so I do not have your last name. So I got a fake certificate from friends I have at the Polish embassy that says we got married there in the embassy only two weeks ago and so could not get our passports changed in time. The certificates are fake and so not legal, but I heard how strict some of these Muslim countries are. I do not want to take any chance. I am not sleeping in a room by myself, or even in a dorm with other women. I am staying with you. Complete time with you. So our passports show no marriage and mine has my single name. For a hotel, if they matter about it, I have a marriage certificate to show so that we can share our room together. Pity my fears, Hunter. Please do not be angry."

"No, I get it, Ewa. I understand. Not only that, it makes me feel good. I love being married to you, even pretend."

She nearly squeezed my hand in appreciation, but brought it back to her side in fear of offending others.

Along the way there were signs on the side of the

road. The lights of our bus flashed upon them. Some of the signs told of a nearby ancient Fire Temple. This perked my interest. Ancient Persia was famous for perhaps the world's first prophet, Zoroaster. These Fire Temples were from that sect, Zoroastrianism. The man was a forerunner to many of the beliefs incorporated into Judaism and thus into Christianity and Islam. Since Persia, under Cyrus and later kings, was a conqueror of Israel, Zoroastrianism proved to be a major influence on much of our belief system. Zoroaster taught free will. He opposed hallucinogenic plants in rituals. He was also against polytheism, over-ritualized religious ceremonies, and animal sacrifices. He also was against the oppressive class system in Persia. He taught about Heaven and Hell, and introduced the concept of resurrection of the body and of the last judgment. He taught that an everlasting life reunited soul and body. The dualism of good versus evil in Zoroastrianism found its way into Judaic thought.

And of course, in the Jewish Tanakh, or Old Testament, is the story of Esther, from which came the Jewish holiday Purim. This story told how the entire Jewish race in the Persian Empire would have been wiped out but for the intervention of the beloved Jewish wife of Xerxes.

Even though I wasn't a religious Jew and didn't take these concepts at face value, I loved the ties between ancient Persia and my Jewish heritage. I belonged here, I decided. I now felt bold. And I was going to take care of Ewa, too.

Karaj was our last stop before Tehran. A man got on the bus and sat just in front of me. He wore a dress shirt and slacks. He kept turning toward us, as if to check us out, then looked back to the front of the bus. Finally, he twisted around enough to talk to me.

"Are you American, by chance?" he asked me.

"Your English is very good," I complimented him.

"Yes, I work at an American firm in Tehran. I am on my way to work now."

"Does that mean we're almost to Tehran, then?" I asked, showing pleasure at the thought.

"Yes, half an hour at the most. Less than that to the city itself. I also studied in America. In Michigan. I am a computer specialist."

"Did you like America?"

"Of course. Very nice place. Friendly people." He then looked intensely at me. "What brings you here, might I ask?"

"I'm on the way to India. I have friends there. I was in Germany and decided I'd like to go overland, see some places I've heard about all my life."

"So you're not staying in Iran, then?"

"No, just passing through."

"That is best," he said. "And I do not mean it in a bad way. I like Americans. Most Iranians do, I suppose. I mean we do, but now things are complicated. There are those that are angry at America. They blame America for many of the problems here. I cannot talk too much about this. But, my friend, I would not stay very long in Tehran. In spite of many friendly people there, it is difficult to say what might happen. Some have strong feelings against America."

"Thank you," I said, smiling at him. "We'll be careful. I won't invite problems."

"Your presence here alone will invite problems with some. I wish you well, my friend."

Soon I saw a city skyline in the distance as the sun began to rise. Tehran. Thank God. I looked at Ewa, and she smiled at me as if to share our joy at the sight. I felt refreshed suddenly. As we got closer, I saw a large tower-looking object, but with an arch in the center of it and with a graduating base tapering into the middle of the tower.

We drove through the city for a while before coming to the bus station. I already worried how far we might have to walk before we found a cheap but good hotel.

"Good luck, my friend," the Iranian in front of me said while getting up from his seat to leave. He then smiled and nodded toward Ewa. "Where will you stay?"

"Are there any cheap hotels nearby?" I asked.

"And clean too," added Ewa.

"Yes, of course. Do not choose the first you see, of course, but after about two blocks they become reasonably priced. And let me warn you. Do not change your money on the streets. There are so many scammers. Also be warned: if the corner of a bill is torn off, it is not worth the full price of the value written on the note. Exchange what money you need at an official bank. And when you are walking on the street, just to be safe, try not to walk in front of a car even if it is parked."

"Thanks," I said as he began to leave. "It was nice to meet you."

Tehran looked as modern as Ankara or Istanbul, not nearly as much as Vienna, but pleasant. The traffic was as bad as that in Istanbul. We felt we were taking our lives into our hands by crossing the streets at times.

I wasn't sure what to expect regarding people's appearances, but since I knew the Shah's Iran was Westernized, I wasn't surprised to see most of the people dressed in American-style clothes. Even Turkey, once we got east of Ankara into the Asian part of the country, had many dressed in robes or loose-fitting trousers. Most women in both countries wore dresses, but those were more colorful and made of thicker material than in Europe.

We found the perfect hotel, reasonably priced, clean, and not too fancy. It even had an attached bathroom. The clerk didn't seem to care if we were married and gave us a room with a nice double-sized bed.

"I am so tired, Hunter, that I just want to sleep. Not bathe, not wash my clothes, just crawl into bed and sleep. I do not care to take off my clothes. I want to crash—such a great American word that sounds perfect for how I feel just now."

And crash we did, on top of the covers and fully clothed. The nippy air outside made us feel all the cozier. As we drifted off to sleep, Ewa placed one hand on my shoulder and another across my chest. She then tugged slightly at my shoulder to get my attention.

"Hunter. I am not trying to tease you. You have been so patient with me. I told you in Istanbul that I wanted to make love to you. That you would be the first for me. Then I did not follow through on this vow to you. But I am experiencing my menstrual cycle now."

I waited for more explanation, but there wasn't more. She then waited for me to say something. I nodded to show I understood. I was even relieved at her explanation. I wanted to make love to her, but I still felt more like her protector, even on this subject. I was willing to live with the complexities of our situation.

It was midafternoon before we got up. Even though I didn't plan on doing much in Tehran, I regretted we were getting such a late start on our one day here, since I intended to go to Isfahan the next day.

We were both hungry, and food was always a good place to start in a new environment. Tehran looked prosperous, and there were abundant restaurants and shops around. We chose one that looked clean and simple. Their food selection resembled what we had seen in Turkey—grilled meats, rice, fresh vegetables, yogurt, and flat bread.

"I really like Asia for the food," Ewa chirped.

"It's not as good as in Turkey, though. Not to me anyway. I like it, and I can't place why I'm making a comment like that, but Turkey's was even better somehow, at least the food we ate in the cities anyway."

"I believe it is the way they cook," Ewa replied. "Turkish was somehow juicier."

"The people look different too," I commented. "Their skin is lighter. Beige instead of dark like in Turkey."

"The Aryans, you know," Ewa answered. "Caucasus Mountains north of here in Russia is where it began. The Aryans went all the way down into India. I know they are darker brown in India, but through the centuries, I suppose, that happened with breeding."

"That's where they got the name for the country," I added. "The word Aryan turned into Iran. I don't know who dreams this stuff up, though. It kind of bugs me. I know it's their business and all, but for millennia you have Persia in all its glory. And then someone gets a better idea."

"You are funny," Ewa said with a giggle. "But yes, Persia sounds more glorious."

A large television was near us, elevated on a stand and attached to the wall. Soon there was a scene of Mecca at a Hajj. The Kaaba stone enhancement had thousands of pilgrims marching in a flow around it. I quit eating to concentrate. The scene thrilled me. I loved the pride and devotion displayed in this scene. There was a unifying spirit that I envied.

Ewa saw my fascination and began to watch with me. We stared until the Hajj scene was completed and then smiled at one another. This scene alone enhanced our travel.

"Do you want to do something special?" I asked her as we finished eating. "Something to see or buy?"

"Not that I can think of. But we are here in Persia, and it is famous for their carpets. I know we cannot buy one and take it around with us, but I would like to find a shop. Just to see."

"That's a good idea. See, there you go again, Ewa. I would have never thought of that, unless I stumbled onto a shop with carpets in it."

And in our touristic part of Tehran, carpet shops were in abundance.

"Can I help you?" A mustachioed man asked me just after we entered a store.

This shop, however, looked more like a warehouse.

"We're just looking," I answered.

The man hadn't smiled the entire time since we entered. Two other men were with him, and they also looked grave and serious. All wore Western-style clothing with collared, pressed, cotton shirts, and creased cotton slacks.

"Do you live here?" The mustachioed man asked me.

"Tourists," I replied.

"We have the ability to send it to your destination for you," the man said, still with a serious expression.

"We prefer just to look for a while," I replied.

We walked around inspecting their carpets. They were pretty, but I didn't care. I had no idea of their quality, and I didn't understand why people cared about these things. I saw a practical use, in that they were rather thick and could either be rolled up and stored or laid on the floor during winter months. If you were going to use one, then it may as well be pretty, I thought.

"Do you see anything that interests you?" another of the men asked me.

I shook my head no. We were the only customers in the store, and I felt as if we were teasing them since we had no intention to buy.

"Are you American?" the third man asked me.

"Yes."

"What brings you here?"

"We're on our way to India, and we wanted to see some of the places in between."

"In between where? America and India?"

"No, we started off in Vienna."

"What will you do in India?"

"I have a contact there. There's a social ashram there, and I wanted to meet them and help in some way and see how they operate."

"So, they are Hindu, then?"

"Yes. But it's not a religious ashram. Sort of like

the Catholic Relief or something."

"The Catholic Relief?"

"A religious charity in America."

"Are you Catholic?" he asked me.

"Yes, we are both Catholic," Ewa answered for me abruptly.

All three men looked at Ewa as if inspecting her.

"Christianity is a good religion," the man talking to me continued. "Islam is the best."

"How long have you been in Iran?" the mustachioed man asked.

"We just got here," I replied. "We'll take a train to Isfahan tomorrow."

"Oh, no," the mustachioed man said with a grimace while shaking his head. "Americans are not welcomed there. It should be safe for you in Tehran, but I would continue on to Pakistan. I would go straight through. Things are tense here because of the Shah."

"We'll only spend a day there," I answered. "It's a historical city, and we'd like to see it. It was twice the capital of ancient Persia and all. But we're going to Afghanistan next, anyway."

"You are either brave or a fool, my friend. Afghanistan also does not like Americans. It has a Communist dictator supported by the Russians. Why do you make such a journey?"

"Yes, I know about Afghanistan. We'll just pass through there too. A few days only."

They all three looked at Ewa, again showing concern.

"Things will not be good for her in Afghanistan. They live in the dark ages."

"We'll just be there for a few days," I repeated.

"Be careful, then. There are some angry people these days. Times are unsure."

I nodded I understood as we turned to leave the store.

"Thanks for intervening for me about religion," I told Ewa as we walked again on the streets of Tehran. "I wasn't worried about them knowing I was Jewish, but you never know, actually. Especially with the mood in Iran seeming so unpredictable."

"Yes, I was worried about you. And even about me if something happened to you. It is best not to take chances."

I wasn't in the mood to window shop anymore. And even though Tehran was Iran's capital city, I didn't feel like visiting any museums or government buildings either. I began looking for restaurants, even though I wasn't hungry.

"Hey," I exclaimed to Ewa. "Look at that."

"What, Hunter?"

"A Jewish room of some sort. There's a menorah against the back wall. A reading room or study room or something. Let's check it out."

"Where?"

"Across the street."

We made our way, jaywalking as we did so. Ewa held my hand as we dodged the traffic. Now was the time to get hit by a car if someone so intended it to happen to two Europeans. And holding hands at that.

"We made it," Ewa celebrated as she let go of my hand.

I opened the door of the shop slowly and looked around. There was indeed a menorah on a counter against the wall, as well as bookshelves, and even a coffeepot. Two young men were reading while sitting on a cushioned couch. One looked up at me curiously.

"I assume y'all are Jewish," I said.

"Yes. So you speak English," one of them said.

"Come sit with us," the other beckoned.

Ewa and I walked to them and sat on an armchair each, both facing them.

"Are you also Jewish?" The first one asked me.

"Yes. From America. My friend here, though, is from Poland. And not Jewish."

"What brings you to Tehran? Do you work for an American firm or for the embassy?"

"No, we're on our way to India. We're just passing through. We're going to Isfahan tomorrow, then Mashhad, on our way to Afghanistan."

"You have it all planned out," the second one said with a smile.

"Qom is on the way to Isfahan," the first one added. "Do you not care?"

"We don't want to spend too much time in Iran. We keep hearing things. We just want to get a quick look and then move on."

I studied them.

"How is it for you here?" I asked them.

"It has been good under the Shah, for Jews," the first one explained. "People are religious here, but it has been a secular country wanting to enter the twentieth century. Before the Shah, there was an Islamic hierarchy where the clergy owned so much of Iran. Between that and strict laws, including about banks and loans on interest, Iran struggled. Even with oil. The Shah opened things up a great deal. He took away much of the hold on power by the Islamists and their hold on property. It has been good overall, but to hold on to power the Shah needed America and England, but also Savak. Savak is the special police. They are ruthless. Much like the SS was under the Nazis. It has made the Shah very unpopular. And, since you asked, we are quite concerned about the future here."

"That's what I keep hearing," I said. "I keep hearing the Shah may even abdicate soon."

They both nodded agreement to that statement.

"I do not see how he can stay in power much longer," one of them explained. "There is already armed resistance, but more than that there is already a government-in-exile in France, waiting to take over once the time is right and the Shah is gone."

"A government-in-exile?" I asked curiously.

"Yes," the first one said. "There is a mullah that is very popular. Not just with the religious zealots, but now with most that want the Shah gone. At first there was approval of the Shah's modernizing. Iran prospered. But he is so ruthless. And corrupt. He has lost much of his support. So this mullah in France is the symbol for even the more secular Muslim in Iran."

"Why have I never heard of him?"

"Perhaps Americans do not find these things out."

"What's his name?"

The second one picked up a pen and wrote something down on a small piece of paper and handed it to me. I read it and tried to form how it must sound.

"Khomeini?" I asked.

Both jerked their heads and looked around nervously.

"Quiet," the first one said. "We are probably bugged, and Savak can hear what you say. To even speak that name may get bad attention for us."

"So what will you do?" I asked them. "If the worst happens."

"Go to Israel," the second one explained. "I suspect things will not go well for the Jews here. Even the moderate Muslims feel a pride that is coming out now. We must see how far this fanatic fervor goes once the genie is out of the bottle. But you two must keep going. You will be safe in Tehran, but beware of Isfahan and especially Mashhad."

I saw the look of concern on Ewa's face. I had to take them seriously, but I was going to these cities.

Chapter 7

Ewa and I took a train direct to Isfahan the next morning. Unbelievably, we found a car with compartments, some of which were empty. For however long we could manage, we would have a compartment all to ourselves.

It was a two-hundred-mile journey from Tehran to Isfahan. This train was an express, which meant, for us, there were few stops and we would arrive by noon.

All I saw was semi-arid bleakness as I looked out the window along the way. Except for a few mountains in the distance, all there seemed to be was an open expanse of dry terrain. There were towns and villages along the way in the middle of this bleakness, but they appeared as just another manifestation of it, as if it were a place of refuge from even starker realities.

Also along the way I saw more signs of Fire Temples. Were any of them still active, I wondered, or just historic relics and museums? I was amazed that, in this Muslim world, there was any sign of prominence of a history, which for all I knew was now considered heretical. I wondered how they would fare when Khomeini came to power.

There was nothing bleak about Isfahan. It not only appeared prosperous but had the exotic architecture and layout I adored. There was a spirit here, an energy. Some of the mosques took my breath away. There were bazaars and city squares, one in particular, the old square, which started at the most glorious mosque of all, the Jāmeh Mosque.

We chose a hotel at the edge of one of their more enchanting bazaars. Our room was clean, reasonably priced, and had a bathroom attached. There was a wonderful double-sized bed in the middle of this room from where we could see the Jāmeh Mosque through our window.

"This was worth our trip," Ewa said with a bright smile. "I feel as if I am in some modern version of Arabian nights. Except Iran is not an Arab country nor are the people Arab. But I do not care. I am a tourist. That is even better. I am in modern-day ancient Persia, instead."

"I want to go to that Jāmeh Mosque," I said. "Just to take an up-close picture of it. To look inside if I can. You never know if they are going to let you. And then we'll just stroll through the courtyard and marketplace."

We were allowed into the courtyard of the mosque, but barely entered. It was enough for me to look at the structure and feel the significance of the place, to take in the designs, and read the Arabic-looking script.

Soon we were back out on the streets and meandering among the shops of the nearby bazaar, except today there was a strike against the Shah, and the shops were closed. I didn't want to buy anything, but the strike made it more difficult to appreciate the flavor of the shops and the atmosphere. I wasn't disappointed, however. I could go window shopping anytime. To be in Iran during a political strike was a special event, so I was glad to be in Isfahan for that.

The strike made getting food more difficult. There

were restaurants open in some places, and I had no idea if they were breaking the strike, but I didn't care, since I was hungry.

"Are you American?" The man behind the counter in the restaurant asked me as he took my order and my money. "Are you not afraid to be on the streets today?"

"Should I be?" I asked him.

"You are safe in Isfahan. People are very friendly and like Americans. But it is a bad time, and there are those that are angry at America for backing the Shah. I would stay in Isfahan. Do not go to Tehran."

"I just came from there. They told me they are friendly there and not to come here."

The man laughed. "How long are you here?"

"We leave tomorrow for Mashhad."

I saw the grimace on his face.

"Don't go there?" I chided him. "It's dangerous there for me?"

He did not laugh this time.

"Yes, my friend. I am sorry to tell you it is dangerous for you there. To make it worse, not tomorrow but after tomorrow there is a holy day. Not Friday, but special holy day. Emotions will be intense. Be very careful, my friend."

After eating, we found it convenient to us that the shops were closed. Since we couldn't look around, it gave us more time to relax. But how much relaxing was I supposed to do in Iran? Everywhere I went there was some kind of warning. We needed to experience something normal. But the problems gave Iran a special flavor for memories.

And now we heard about Mashhad—Mashhad, the holy city, and we would be there on a holy day. It also had a famous mosque. Was I supposed to miss all that?

"Where is it we go tomorrow?" Ewa asked as we sipped coffee at yet another restaurant. "This place we were warned not to go?"

"Mashhad," I replied. "It is east, but also back north. Near the Soviet Union, at least their southern Muslim countries, and also Afghanistan."

"So we go to Afghanistan. I heard you talk about it before. You seem to do this because of your desires, not for mine. I did want to show you Eastern Bloc Bulgaria. And I do want to see this Soviet puppet, Communist Afghanistan, but you are doing it because of you. We even go out of our way to go there. You want to see everything, not just experience a bit of India and a country or two along the way. This is more than adventure. You are hungry to see things."

I shrugged my shoulders, then nodded. I saw the look of confusion on her face, so I decided this was a good time to explain more about our trip.

"I don't fit anywhere, Ewa, so I want to do all this adventure stuff. But it's more than that, just like you said. I need historic reference stuff. America has lost its soul. There's a lot there I love, but I'm struggling for answers right now. Plus, I just want to see things. I'll settle down someday, join the consumer society, but I need to get some bearing first."

"You seem like a hippie the way you are talking. I thought you hated hippies."

"Not really. Well, yes, I do. They seem phony to me. It's more a party for them than a cause. And I don't like their value system. Drugs, sex, and rock-and-roll values. They want a revolution and think somehow they should run it. They claim to hate the rat race and how they want to get back to nature, but they weren't up to it, as it turns out. Surprise, surprise, surprise. Hippies are just a new religion, a cult. They knocked the rest of America for being hypocrites, but that's what they are. I know it's more complicated than that. But John Lennon was right in the song 'Revolution,' about how they had better free their minds instead. Even if they think they've got the answer better than what America has already accomplished, which they don't, they still have to know how to implement that answer."

"You are so angry."

"I have a chip on my shoulder, I know it. And actually, I like some of the hippie ideas. The rat race got to me too. I don't hate the rat race per se, but I hate being stuck with it. But it brought prosperity and education and opportunity. I don't trust a hippie to accomplish more than what we've already got in our lives and system, and that includes how screwed up we are in the mix. Anyway, materialism alone got to me, including the materialism of the so-called hippies. Racism sucks, and a lot of cops and politicians are indeed corrupt or inept. And so what? Hippies aren't? They know how to correct it all better than what we're doing? They're more insightful? They sure want to think so. We already have the mechanisms to help us through if we just free our minds instead. We don't need a bunch of spoiled brats that seldom had to work or sacrifice or fix anything. And hippies need money, as it turns out, as much as the rats in the rat race. But they think they need it to buy their freedom rather than to free themselves inside."

I saw her trying to follow all I was saying. Could I explain all this to anyone, much less a girl from another world than mine?

"You are ranting, Hunter."

I acknowledged with a nod.

"I just didn't fit in back home," I explained again. "I got a job in Houston in computers for a year, and I was so miserable. I wanted to settle down, and I enjoyed the prosperity and security. But actually, emotionally, I hated all that. It was like my life was all placed and snug and directed. So, things I liked about hippies—their ideas to break away, to look at different aspects of life and live simply, open up to new cultures and ideas—all that had an appeal to me. So why am I making this trip? The Beatles got everyone excited about India, and I like the Orient anyway, ever since I was a boy, and when I was in the Marines. Hindu and Buddhist philosophy has an appeal, from the outside, anyway. When I meet any Hindus or Buddhists and look into anything about them, they are just as human and stuck as Jews and Christians. But I like some of the philosophy and music. So I want to breathe some new air while I have the chance. I came across a book about going overland to Katmandu, and it sounded great— overland, not flying. Don't jetset it. Take it one country at a time. And, speaking of hippies, we're on what is called the Hippie Trail to India. There are two of them, actually. From here we can go south and east into Pakistan. But we're going east and north to Afghanistan. And from there south through the Khyber Pass into Pakistan. The Khyber Pass, just like Rudyard Kipling!"

"I can say many of the things you say, Hunter, in my own way. It is so oppressive in my country, so hypocritical. But it is my country. There is much to hate, and I do hate many things in my country. This structure of the rat race, as you describe—I know Poland is different from America, but I live in my own rat race. Yet there is much happening there now, exciting things. The trade unions are angry in Poland. There is never enough money. Working conditions are oppressive. There is anger at people like my father. I too have to get my bearings. Polish people are defying their government. That concerns me, but it excites me. The Catholic Church is also angry. The new Pope from Poland gives us courage. There is hope and devotion for change."

I nodded yes in sympathy to her.

"You make me ashamed, Ewa. You're the one that has it so bad."

"But also not so bad. My father is part of the power structure. I have privileges many do not have. But still I want to know other things and to see other things. Just like you. Even because of you, now. I want to try to understand more about my country by understanding more about life. You and I are alike in wonderful ways. We will have to deal with going back to our countries someday, but first we need to understand more. Is this fate, Hunter? That we are here together in our search? Sharing our search?"

"It's spooky, isn't it," I said with a smirk. "I do believe that about fate, I think. It's just that I shouldn't."

"And why should we not believe in fate? What do we know? So search with me. Share with me. Question our fate, but not that there is fate, the fate given to us for now."

"I'm glad you weren't brought up religiously," I

commented.

"Oh, but I am religious now, in my way. I am even Catholic religious sometimes. I just do not understand so many things."

"You know what I like about you, Ewa," I said, as she smiled at my words.

"What, Hunter? What is it you like so about me?"

"Go ahead and be Catholic. But don't overdo it. Because you have a hunger inside you that I adore. And it's so beyond the structured church. Don't ever let belief in God overtake your search for God. And never let a need for answers be more important than the need to question."

"Are you a guru, Hunter?" she asked me with a laugh. "Is this why we go to India on this Hippie Trail of yours? I have no clue what you just said, my dear man. But thank you anyway."

"I'm no guru," I replied, ready to blush. "But I think about life a lot. My values belong back in World War II. Courage, hard work, surviving, duty. Doing what it takes. It seems like the hippies just take the opposite stance. At first there was some fresh thought with them. We lived such a structured life in Western society. That's normal and needed. Structure and values. But life is so complicated, and in an open and democratic place like America, other ideas are going to come out. Good. And there will be resistance to it. So what. Bring it on. Because some ideas are bad ones. Some are even evil. Some are ideas whose time has come, though. I love that part. But even then these new good ideas have to be implemented, worked out, and adjusted to. When I heard some of these new, questioning ideas about racism or Vietnam, Capitalism versus Socialism, I loved so many of these questions that came from hippies. But I love how I was raised, too, and I'm right because of it. I didn't mind seeing my values challenged so much as watching all the stupid pied pipers taking advantage of the chaos. And there weren't many deep thinkers in my generation after all. They sure thought so when they took the other side about something. But that's all most of them did. Just followed another side religiously. Religion has its hypocrisy and bigotry, but it's worked out a lot of wisdom, too, and depth. If you're going to be a follower, you're going to take in the faults with the good values. But when you rebel against religion, it doesn't mean you've figured anything out. You sure don't learn much in just rebelling. What's your follow-through? That's the key. Most people don't have one."

I looked at her apologetically.

"I get on a roll," I said meekly. "But that's why I'm here doing all this. Since you asked, ha. I love adventure, but I need answers. And there's always more questions than answers."

She reached over to hold my hand.

"There is a fate, Hunter. I need all this too, and then I met you and here we are."

I nodded appreciation for her understanding.

"And tonight I am ready for you," she continued. "I want to make love to you. The one who shares my fate and now my search."

The blunt, honest way she presented herself to me put a lump in my throat. She knew what she wanted, and it was me. The thought of making love to her excited me, but it also felt like a responsibility. I didn't want to fail her.

There was diminished sunlight in the November sky in Isfahan as we made our way to our hotel room. To our destination. I pulled the curtain to make the room as dark as possible. Only a trace of light remained, which provided a tease and an allure. As I did so, Ewa methodically took off her clothes. She lay in bed as I disrobed, then reached out both her arms to me as I crawled in next to her. We embraced, kissed, then looked at the traces of shadows we were to one another.

I could see the trust in her eyes and the longing. I felt a tenseness about her, the unknowns I was sure she had to deal with. The physical awkwardness and pain a woman who is a virgin encounters is not pleasant. This put a damper on things for me. But the trust in her eyes was worth everything. She would remember me for the rest of her life, and I was grateful.

And for the first time I told her, "I love you, Ewa," as we kissed.

She looked at me as if searching for words.

"I have loved you since Wien. I was afraid it was silly of me. But now we are here. We are here and in love."

Chapter 8

We took the express train to Mashhad, and once again it was only partially filled. Happily we claimed an empty compartment for ourselves.

After two stops, however, three men entered our compartment to share it. All three were bearded, with black, bushy hair touching their ears. They had darker brown skin than most Iranians, and their clothes were like none we had seen before. Their long-sleeved shirts were loosely fitting, with a column of buttons to the side over the pectoral region. Their trousers were rugged and baggy. They barely smiled as they entered our compartment and sat directly across from us, studying us as they did so. Soon they concentrated their stares toward Ewa. She nervously inched closer to me.

I nodded a greeting their way and with a half smile they nodded back. After a few minutes, one of them placed several pieces of candy, glossed like polished rocks, onto the windowsill near me. Each of the three men leaned over occasionally to grab a piece to savor in their mouths. One looked at me and nodded politely toward the candy as if offering me a piece. In defiance of my discomfort around them, I grabbed a handful of the candy, tore off the paper coverings roughly, and popped them into my mouth, crunching them as if eating peanuts.

All three men looked at me angrily.

I smirked contempt and gazed out the window.

Their anger increased.

I let my lack of concern show on my face.

"We go to Mashhad," Ewa blurted out to them nervously.

The three men stared at her again, their animosity unappeased.

"Do you speak English?" Ewa asked them meekly in slow, deliberate words.

"I speak little English," the one directly across from me said to her.

"Wonderful," she said with an overly polite smile. "How do you know English?"

"I work before on American military base in Bahrain."

"Are you from Mashhad?"

"We are Afghani," the man said.

"Afghani?" Ewa asked.

He nodded.

"I never met anyone from Afghanistan. How wonderful."

They kept staring at her as if scoping her out. She then looked at me crossly.

"If you are hungry, you will not fill your appetite from these candy pieces. Do not do such a rude thing again."

The man nearest the door of the compartment reached into his bag and pulled out a can of something. He opened it and offered it to his two Afghan companions. They grabbed pieces from it and stuffed them into their mouths. The man offering them looked at me as if planning to offer but then decided against it.

"What is that?" Ewa asked, to ease the still-prevalent tension.

"Tabak," the English-speaking one replied.

"Oh, you mean snuff?" Ewa asked while breaking into an approving smile.

"Snuff, yes. Snuff."

Ewa then reached into her backpack to retrieve a can the size and shape of a hockey puck.

"Look, I also have snuff," she said, showing the container to them.

I looked at her in disbelief.

"What are you doing with snuff?" I asked her.

"It is for my father. He loves it. When I go to Wien I always buy for him. It is high quality. I even like to smell it."

She then offered the container to the three men.

"Here, take it. I have more."

The three of them smiled at her. The one across from her took the snuff, opened the can, inspected it, and began to smell it. Even brighter smiles of appreciation spread on their faces. They even smiled at me. I smiled back, thinking Ewa just may have saved our lives.

"I'll behave," I promised her.

"We go back Afghanistan," the English speaker said. "We work build road Iran and now go back money for families. Why you go Mashhad? You are American?"

"Yes, we're American," I answered.

"Why go you Mashhad? Not good for you."

"We're going to India and want to stop in Mashhad," I answered.

"You go next Afghanistan?"

"Yes," I answered.

"You go with us. From Mashhad we go over mountains to Afghanistan. We no work visa here. We go back Afghanistan, back Iran, back Afghanistan, over mountains. You go with us."

I pictured it and loved the idea.

"We will get in trouble," Ewa interjected nervously. "We are white, and if we get caught it is very bad for us."

The Afghan nodded his head that he understood.

"We show you how live in Afghanistan. Good people. We show you."

"Thank you so much," she answered. "We would love to go to your village. But we must go to Herat." She looked at me inquisitively. "Herat, right? Isn't that the first stop for us? Near the border?"

I nodded yes. "It's a bit inland, actually," I explained.

"So we should not break Afghan laws," she said apologetically. "Good people in Afghanistan, and we do not want to break any laws."

The man nodded yes again.

"Where you stay Mashhad?" The man asked.

"Hotel," I answered.

"We go hotel there. We take you. Little money for hotel. We show you. We show you bus for Herat."

We were all friends now, thanks to Ewa's snuff, and felt cozy with one another. Occasionally one of them broke out flat bread or fruit to offer us, a reassurance of our bond with one another along the trip.

It was early afternoon before we arrived in Mashhad. We were tired, but our Afghan friends delivered on their promise to find us cheap lodging, when we followed them. Not far from the station was a hostel that included separate rooms. The Afghanis took a room next to ours. Our room was clean but small, even smaller than what we had in Sofia, made of wood and with two single cots. Ewa and I immediately pushed the two cots together, but the borders were so pronounced that it was impossible to sleep together as in one bed.

"Do you want to walk around first?" I asked Ewa. "There's a communal shower in the hostel here, one for each gender, where we can freshen up and wash our clothes."

"Let us walk about first," she replied. "I am hungry. Surely you are too."

"I can wait if you want to shower first."

We heard a tap on our door. It was our English-speaking friend.

"Have you hungry?" he asked me.

"Yes," we answered in unison.

"We take you to food. You come with us. Mashhad no good for Americans. Careful."

It felt good to have a guide. And halfway around the world, it felt good to have local friends. So we took them up on the food search.

"Meat," is all we said to our friend as we sat at a table in a small restaurant.

"Rice? Yogurt? Bread?" Our friend offered choices.

"It all sounds good."

I was still talking slowly to make sure he understood. It was habit by now.

It was fun to watch them eat. They dove in. The slices of meat they wrapped with pieces from the flat bread. The rice they scooped with their hands and jammed into their mouths. Only with their yogurt did they bother to use a spoon.

"Is there a mosque here?" I asked after the meal, wanting to make small talk while we sipped on our coffee. I already knew that Mashhad had a beautiful mosque.

"Yes. But special mosque. For dead imam. Tomb mosque. Tomorrow special day for Imam Reza."

"Tomorrow?" I asked perking up. "Great. Perfect. We'll wait and go tomorrow, then."

"No," our friend said emphatically. "You not go tomorrow. Much anger to Americans. Danger for you. Danger for Afghanis. Afghani Sunni, Iran Shiite. We go Afghanistan tomorrow. Danger for you here now. You go with us."

I didn't argue, but I was going to the mosque. I wanted to see the special event tomorrow.

"So you want to just walk around?" I asked Ewa. "Then wash up?"

She nodded as we got up to leave.

"*Ciao*," she said to them on the way out. "See you at the hostel."

We were afraid to walk around much, for fear of getting lost. There was a bazaar near our hostel, and we were satisfied with that. Just to get a feel of Mashhad was all we needed. The big event would be the pilgrimage tomorrow at the tomb. That would be our special Mashhad memory. Then on to Afghanistan.

"An English-speaking newspaper," Ewa pointed out at a news counter in the bazaar.

I was sure it would be the international newspaper from America, the one we read in Ankara, but no, it was out of Tehran for the American and British companies and staff working in Iran. Curious, we bought it to read when we got back to our hostel.

There was no wall heater in our room to dry our hand-washed clothes, so we used the last bit of sunlight shining through the window in our room. Surely, they would be dry by the time we left for the border tomorrow at noon.

"Hunter," Ewa said, showing concern as she read the newspaper while we lay in bed. "We cannot go to that pilgrimage tomorrow."

I wanted to roll my eyes. Yet another warning.

"This is a very sacred imam in Persian history. This man was a descendent of Muhammad. But that is not our concern. The problem with us going tomorrow is that he is a symbol. Not just religious but political. When the Shah's family became ruler before World War II, they tried to modernize Iran."

"Like the current Shah is trying to do."

"Yes. But listen. That's the problem, if you remember. The modernization and power struggle. But in particular about this shrine and the pilgrimage tomorrow and now about us going, there was already a rebellion right here at this shrine in 1935. There were modernization reforms, but also corruption, and high taxes. Many of the people here rebelled and took over the shrine we intend to go to. The Iranian army refused to fire on the shrine."

"That's what is already happening in parts of the country," I countered. "They say it's getting close to where the military won't follow orders from the Shah. That's why the Shah will probably be leaving soon. Before the grand mutiny."

"The Shah back then in 1935 used foreign troops."

"I hope not American."

"From Azerbaijan. They were willing to attack the shrine and stop the rebellion. That's why tomorrow is so significant. This memory is special to them tomorrow, now that Khomeini waits for the army to rebel against the Shah. The newspaper says that Americans are being warned in Mashhad to not even be on the streets tomorrow." She paused for emphasis. "How can we even go to the bus to leave tomorrow, much less go to this shrine? I am frightened, Hunter."

It sounded serious, but instead of scaring me, it pissed me off. Another threat to defy.

I took the newspaper from her and began to read on my own. But as soon as I read something that put fear into me, the defiant part of me came out to counter it.

But it said much more than frightening things.

"It says this mosque," I explained, "this shrine mosque complex, is the largest in the whole world. God, I've got to see this, Ewa. Our one chance. And on a holy day, too."

"No, Hunter. You cannot do this. You cannot be serious."

"I'll go alone. Just in case."

"They mean it, Hunter. It talks of harm, even killing of Americans. They mean it. Please listen to me, Hunter."

"Let's go to sleep. See how we feel in the morning."

"I cannot make love tonight, Hunter. Not now. The bed is a problem anyway, but now I am scared. I am so frightened. Let me just hold your hand for reassurance."

Early the next morning there was a knock on our door. As I got up to open it, Ewa cautioned that it may be a trick.

"Who?" I asked through the door to the outside.

Ewa and I began to get dressed as I talked.

"Friend," answered the voice.

I opened it. All three of our Afghan friends were staring at me as I did so.

"We have you bus for Herat," our English speaker said immediately. "You stay in room before go. No go outside. Bus leave noon. We go with you to bus."

"That's so sweet of you," Ewa said. She rushed over to them, and I thought at first she was going to hug them, but she shook each one's hand instead.

"First I want to go to the mosque," I told them.

"No, no," our friend replied harshly. "You not go. It very bad for you. You not go."

"I just want to see some of it," I said as I began to walk past them.

"Hunter!" Ewa shouted at me as she followed me out the door. "Hunter," she repeated as she hugged me. "Please, please do not do this. Do not go, my love."

I returned her embrace.

"I won't be long, Ewa. I'll be okay. I just want to see what's going on. If it looks bad for me, I'll leave. If not, I still won't be long. We'll make the bus easily. Just pack and wait for me."

"You do not understand. You understand nothing. Is this how Marines are? Are they all crazy? This is not brave. This is insane. To die for nothing."

"Ewa, please understand how much this means to me."

"Then I am going with you. You will not die alone."

"Ewa, don't."

She broke her embrace from me and walked on ahead into the grassy area in front of the hostel. I caught up with her and walked past her.

I had barely gotten into the yard when I was surrounded by angry Iranians.

"Are you American?" One of them shouted at me.

"Americans!" Another one near him shouted.

My Afghani friends were not far behind and rushed to our rescue. They said something to the group of men surrounding us, then pulled at me and Ewa to escort us to our room.

I was scared, a fear that overruled any defiance which would dare to pressure me to my insane mission.

Ewa held onto me while we walked, as if braving a rainstorm, her arms wrapped around my waist, and her head bent down looking at the ground. Our Afghani friends went inside our room with us and sat on the floor near the door to make sure I didn't try to return outside. Soon, one left for the marketplace and brought back bread and meat slices for us to eat. We waited until just before noon. Two of our friends walked in front of us and one at the rear, all the way to the bus station. One of them went to a monitor standing in front of a Volkswagen van, broke out his money belt, and paid the man for our rides to Herat.

"You afraid go mountains to our village, but you not afraid to die in mosque," our friend laughed as he handed me our bus tickets.

All three of them hugged us and walked us to the van.

"Good-bye," Ewa said as we crawled into the van. "Friends. Afghanistan our friends."

"Thank you," I said swelling with gratitude as well

as shame for my persistent insanity.

All three waved at us before walking away.

"I'm supposed to be the one protecting you," I said meekly to Ewa. "That's why you came with me. To be able to travel and be protected. But it's you protecting me from myself. First with the snuff with our friends, and now here in Mashhad."

"Somehow the war inside you is still strong, Hunter," she said looking at me with sympathetic eyes. "Always a Marine has meaning, I suppose."

I shook my head in dismay, thinking about it.

"You touched me," I said. *"Greater love hath no man than to give his life for his friends.* Where I went to college, we have that quote from the Bible on one of our buildings dedicated to our war dead. I have an uncle listed among those war dead." I looked at her, hoping every ounce of devotion I felt for her was evident. "Your name wouldn't be listed on that building, but you were going to die with me. Because of me and with me."

"It took that to get you to care about what you were doing."

I nodded and turned away, revealing the disgust I felt for myself.

More and more people got into our van. We were at the back, since we were the first ones on it. They squeezed us so tightly I could not stretch out my legs or even put my arms to my sides. As the van departed, I counted. Besides the driver, there were twenty-six of us in that VW van. Welcome to Afghanistan.

Chapter 9

The one thing that kept me intact on our cramped-as-sardines seven-hour trip to Herat was the imagery I derived from the overland journey. It wasn't supposed to be easy, and it was the very unease of all this that made things so appealing to me, even to romantic proportions. I was in my own adventure movie in my mind.

As small as Ewa was, she barely fit in the can where we rode, called a VW van. We weren't even able to read. To tweak at the ironies I already felt, we couldn't even hold hands, which would have saved at least a centimeter or more of precious cabin space. We were the only white-skinned Westerners on the trip. Surely, as godless as we were probably already considered by the masses with us, such a bold and lewd sexual expression as holding hands might have gotten us stoned, for all we knew. So we sat quietly, staring out the windows at the same dry, bland scene. An occasional hill or mountain managed to enhance our otherwise miserable and cramped existence. There wasn't even music as there usually was on the bigger buses.

Afghanistan was a Communist country inside the Soviet orbit. It was not part of the USSR, such as Azerbaijan was, but it had recently installed a Russian puppet government. Though our only checkpoint was at the border entering the country, security was very tight due to the tentacles of a police state.

When we arrived in Herat, we encountered a police checkpoint at the bus station. I broke out my passport to the appropriate page, showing my valid Afghan visa stamp. As I prepared for anti-American treatment, the customs officer decided to check Ewa's passport first.

"You are from Poland?" he asked with surprise.

"Yes, I am from Warsaw. My father there is an official."

"Please, please," the man said excitedly. "You must come with me. And your husband also. Follow, please."

The man led us through the crowd into a cordoned-off section of the building. He said something to an assistant, who then rushed off.

"You are my special guests," he said cheerfully. "Poland and the Afghani people are united in friendship. We will give you special favors. You are our guests. Welcome."

Ewa and I looked at one another as we eased into a cautious smile. Soon the assistant returned and placed two cushioned chairs next to us.

"Be seated," the officer instructed. "We will take care of your passports and find a hotel for you in our city."

As we sat, he got to my passport and saw that it was American. A disconcerted look formed on his face as he stared at me.

"What brings you here, American?" he asked sharply.

"He is my husband," Ewa explained. She reached inside her backpack to retrieve our false marriage certificate. "Here," she said handing him the papers. "We were married just before we left Wien. Perhaps you know of it as Vienna. Notice the official Polish embassy seal on our marriage certificate. We met as students there. He is a very enlightened American. My father is chief of the largest construction company in Poland. We intend to go to Poland soon. My husband will assist my father. Until then, there is diplomatic protocol that we must adhere to, until we can renew our passports with our countries to show our recent marriage."

The man looked confused. The information was coming at him too quickly.

"Where is your ultimate destination?" The officer asked while inspecting her papers.

"India," Ewa replied. "We are to meet social workers. Similar to the Red Crescent. India has a long and friendly relationship with Russia, as you know. As part of our honeymoon, we want to visit acquaintances I have there. But not just to visit. We will work in brotherhood there, helping the poor in this pro-Russian socialist country. It will give us a chance to see parts of India, not just come and be imperialistic tourists."

He put the papers aside and stared at Ewa, as if still trying to understand all she was saying. He began nodding his head approvingly.

"Very well. Very good. Very good."

He then looked at me.

"And you are willing to forsake your imperialistic country?"

"As you can see," I said as straight-faced as possible, "I grew to love this beautiful woman who is now my wife. I will not forsake my country, but there is much to work out, and we intend to do so. I will go with her soon to Poland and work with her father. There is much to work out, as I said, but these are our intentions, and I trust it will be arranged as planned. We hope to bridge some gaps of misunderstanding."

The man nodded his head some more, approvingly.

"That is well. Because you are married to her, we will honor your bond with her. Your visa to Afghanistan is legal, and I will honor it. But first, stay in our fair city. Enjoy yourself in a nice hotel we have. It is not a hotel for diplomats, but it is one of our better hotels where people on business often stay. Please do so at our expense, as friends."

He spoke more with his assistant, who then motioned for us to follow him.

"Farewell and good luck," the officer said to us as we left.

I chuckled along the way as I walked next to Ewa.

"What is so funny, my darling husband?" she asked chirpily.

"I'm so glad you allowed me to tag along with you to India. I feel so safe with you."

The hotel where we were driven was near the town center. It was nice, but not luxurious. We were given two free nights to stay, but we chose to use only one.

Travel through this country was primitive. Though it had highways and buses, the highways were narrow, and even the major ones were not in great shape. It would take three days to get through Afghanistan; that was enough to satisfy us. Kandahar would require us to dip quite far south as well as eastward, then back north and eastward to get to Kabul, the capital. We would spend a night in each city, and parts of a day in each.

So Herat we abused, in that it felt so good to be staying in a decent hotel, where we chose to cheat on our adversity with sudden good fortune. We were drawn to wallow in this grandeur and forsake our Hippie Trail mindset for a day, but no more than that. The hotel even machine-washed our clothes for us. It had its own restaurant, which included Western cuisine. We would get plenty of Afghan food along our journey, so we felt like spoiling ourselves for once and eating things from back home that we missed.

"I will wear my nice dress and shoes to the restaurant," Ewa said joyfully. "At last I can feel fancy."

The most glorious part was having a queen-size double bed. No pushing our beds together, no lying at angles or plugging the cracks of joined beds with blankets for comfort. This was the honeymoon we'd longed for. And we had not made love since Isfahan, our only night, in fact, of doing so.

"I do not remember anymore what I fantasized about lovemaking," Ewa said as we lingered in the dark that night. "I could never imagine how wonderful it is. Even in Isfahan, when it was my first time. It was important to me, but important like a rite of passage— to move on in my life as a woman, to experience, and to choose my partner for this rite of passage. Lovemaking is the most wonderful experience in the world. Nothing is more precious than a woman and a man in love and sharing that love."

She stroked my cheek tenderly and kissed me deeply. Soon we were asleep.

****

The bus to Kandahar was not crowded. It was a

81

full-sized bus, and though filled to capacity, it did not have the cramped, stuffy arrangement that we had suffered going to Herat. Exotic oriental music played from the speakers. This was the best part of the ride.

But they separated the men from the women. Men took the front of the bus, while the women were forced to the rear. A thick rope separated the two groups. This annoyed Ewa and me no end. I sat in the very last row of seats provided for the men, while Ewa sat in the seat directly behind me.

Perhaps even worse than not getting to sit next to one another was the physical act of segregation itself. I wanted to be understanding of another culture, but I saw myself judging them, nevertheless. The women not only had to sit at the back of the bus, which I assumed was done condescendingly at their expense, but most women on the bus wore burkas.

A burka is an outer garment worn by women in many Islamic societies in order to cover themselves in public. The face-veiling portion is usually a rectangular piece of semi-transparent cloth with its top edge attached to a portion of the headscarf so the veil hangs down covering the face. The veil resembled a thickly corded mosquito net. It hampers the woman's breathing and even causes lung problems. To me, the women looked subdued in them.

The road to Kandahar was especially dry, much of it through barren desert. As much as we had enjoyed our stay in the nice hotel the night before, I was glad to experience the rugged side of our journey again, in the real Afghanistan, as I pictured things in my mind. I wanted to live closer to the way the locals lived rather than like a tourist.

We found a hostel near the station in Kandahar, where we had to use our false wedding certificate to obtain a room together. The hostel had dormitory-type areas as well as separate rooms, cheap, simple rooms with only beds in them. Even occupants of these rooms had to share communal bathrooms and showers separated by gender.

After pushing our beds together, we went straight to sleep even though it was the middle of the afternoon. We crashed fully clothed, with no energy for anything but holding hands as we did so. The days were getting shorter. We hoped to catch some of Kandahar before twilight, but our fatigue demanded attention first.

"We can wash tonight," Ewa said as we got up from our nap. "They have heating. We can lay out our wet clothes on the windowsill next to it. They should be dry by the morning."

With every country we'd travelled in since we left Austria, the farther south we went, the poorer it got. Afghanistan was by far the poorest country we had been in so far. The Communist takeover during the Saur Revolution seven months earlier couldn't have made things this poor so suddenly, I surmised. As we walked, exploring the town, the shops were small and simple, with very few goods or variety. It was as if there was a trade union ban on selling more than a few different types of goods, to protect equally poor adjoining shops. Many times there weren't even shops but simply open air displays of the wares, spread out on an area of ground only a few square feet in size.

There were many brass items. We walked by countless numbers of them and saw no customers, only men sitting on the ground tinkering on them with small hammers.

Soon we came upon a residential area. The houses were small and poor by Western standards but prosperous compared with what we had seen until now in other parts of the city. Out in the yard of one was a white-skinned girl. She not only had white skin equal in shade to mine and Ewa's, but her mannerisms and aura seemed genuinely American. She looked our age. She wore a loose-fitting local-style dress, but even that didn't cover up her American demeanor. Her thick black-rimmed glasses added to her American looks.

As Ewa and I approached her, she stopped what she was doing and stared at us.

"Are you American?" she asked us in disbelief as we entered her yard area.

"Yes," I replied.

"What are you doing here?" she asked me.

"I should be asking you. We're just passing through. Do you live here?"

She nodded yes.

"Okay," I said with a laugh. "Explain that to me. Why? How?"

She laughed in return.

"I was on my way to India," she began. "Is that where you two are headed?"

Ewa and I both nodded yes.

"I knew it. So many are doing that. I got here last April, just days before the Communist takeover. I got stuck, as a matter of fact, because of it. I couldn't cash any traveler's checks or anything. I met a guy, an Afghani who spoke English. He studied before in England, and that's why he spoke English. He was visiting his family here. They own this house."

She turned toward the house, squinted, smiled, and waved for someone to join her in the yard with us.

"This is my husband," she said wearing a grin as he approached. "We fell in love and I stayed. I help with the family business, which is construction. I help with the bookkeeping."

"You know accounting?" I asked. "Where?"

"NYU. That's New York University, just in case you don't know."

"So you're from New York, then?" I asked.

"Brooklyn, to be exact."

"Brooklyn. You know, you look Jewish, and now you're saying you're from Brooklyn."

"How would you know about Brooklyn and Jews?" she asked, enthused. "You sound like you're from down south. What do you know of Brooklyn?"

"I'm Jewish. Every American Jew probably knows about Jews and Brooklyn."

She studied me curiously.

"You don't look Jewish to me."

"Well, I am," I replied.

"Where are you from, then?"

"Texas."

"I suppose. I guess that's possible. Houston or something."

"Nope. Rural."

"A rural Texas Jew. I repeat, you don't look Jewish to me. Blond-haired and blue-eyed. Are you Ashkenazi or something?"

"I'm sure of it, but I don't know. I'm just Jewish."

"Okay. And you're headed now to India. Why? To find enlightenment? That's so Jewish, I have to admit. These days, anyway."

"No, but I want to see what all the hubbub is about. I had a friend who gave me an address, and what the hell, here I am, talking to a Jew from Brooklyn, New York, in Kandahar."

"Who'd a thunk, huh?" she said with a laugh.

"So why are you still here?" I asked. "You can go home now. I guess you know that."

"It's a bit more complicated than that. Like I say, I'm married now. I had to survive the Communist takeover, for one thing. I didn't particularly feel threatened for my safety, but it was chaotic, and I felt somewhat threatened. Even when I met my hubby here and his family. Then we fell in love and decided to get married. They're traditional here, and I had to pass muster first. American, Jewish, and all that. But his family is modern and educated, and we worked it out. The problem is my family. They wanted me to marry a good Jewish boy back home. Instead, here I am married to a Muslim, and a dark-skinned foreign Muslim on top of that. My family is modern too, so they won't disown me, but I still have some explaining to do, and I haven't gotten to it yet."

"So you're happy here, then?"

She looked over at her husband with a starry-eyed glare that seemed forced to me.

"Very much so," she said as she touched his cheek affectionately with her hand.

Her starry-eyed expression increased and focused straight into his eyes. It seemed phony. If so, was she trying to convince herself she had done the right thing, or was she just another superficial brat of my generation looking for new-age enlightenment, or at least a controversy to soothe her own ego?

"Well, we're leaving tomorrow for Kabul," I told her. "We'd better head back to our hotel and get a good night's rest. It's a long haul."

"Does your friend speak?" The girl asked me while staring at Ewa.

"Yes, I do," Ewa replied with a chuckle. "I did not care to interfere with two Americans."

"You have an accent. So where are you from?" the girl asked her.

"Poland."

"Poland? Are you Jewish? Even after Hitler there's some Jews there?"

"No, I am Catholic."

"I'm almost glad. You also don't look Jewish at all. I was beginning to feel out of place."

Ewa and I smiled at her joke and walked away.

"Ciao," Ewa said with a wave as she turned back toward the girl while we walked.

"Hey, wait," the girl yelled out. "Come back for a second."

We walked back to her.

"I suppose by now," she said with a mischievous grin, "you'd like some toilet paper."

Ewa's eyes lit up, and I'm sure mine probably did too.

"Do you have some?" Ewa swooned at the thought.

"I'm not trying to tease, but no." The girl laughed. "I mostly was sharing. You know, misery-loves-company-style sharing. And there won't be any wherever you're headed, either. You know to use your left hand, yes?"

We understood vividly what she meant. In southern Asia they don't use toilet paper, they use water.

Meaning they dip their hand, apparently the left hand, in water to wipe themselves after dirtying themselves from the toilet.

"And," she continued, "if someone tries to shake your hand using the left hand, they are purposely insulting you. You're foreigners, so you're not supposed to know. They think they get a free insult, so beware, I suppose."

Ewa and I looked at one another and shook our heads in disgust.

The trip to Kabul the next day was just as long and hard as the one to Kandahar from Herat. Again we had to ride with women at the rear of the bus and men at the front. We managed to sit in seats just one row apart again, but this made me want to get out of Afghanistan as soon as possible. Nothing made me judge different customs as much as this inconvenience of being apart from Ewa, even as close as we still got to sit with one another.

The terrain improved along the way to Kabul, however. More and more hills, then mountains greeted us as we drove. Overall, the areas were still very arid. Afghanistan was a fascinating country, but I was glad we were leaving for Pakistan the next day.

Our hostel in Kabul didn't even have a shower. We were given a small room with two cots for beds and no window in it. There was no use of a shower room, just a hole in the floor of bathrooms segregated by gender. To shower we were given a bucket that was filled with water. For an extra twenty cents they warmed the water for us by placing a heated electrical rod in it. We were given a rusty coffee can to dip into this water to pour over our heads and bodies. There would be no washing of our clothes this night.

All we chose to see of Kabul was afforded by a stroll near our hostel. The food was wonderful and saved the day for us, emotionally, as our one real joy. We had shaved meat with rice and flat bread as usual, and the meat was juicier than in any place since Turkey.

****

We were ever so ready for the subcontinent, beginning with Pakistan. The drive through the Khyber Pass, just after crossing the border into Pakistan, was a supercharged thrill for me. It seemed the most exotic place on earth as I pictured all I had read in history and in stories by Rudyard Kipling. Jagged hills and mountains saturated the border just inside Pakistan. The highway sometimes was only one lane wide. It was rugged terrain, but that's what made it the Khyber Pass. It was the romance of the ages that appealed to me, not the hills and mountains themselves. There was a ruggedness to the tribal people who lived there. Many of them were supposedly bandits.

The Khyber Pass satisfied my taste for Pakistan. Instead of three days travelling through Pakistan, like we had given each Asian country up until now, one night in Lahore seemed plenty for us before moving on to India itself. This part of Pakistan was narrow in the north and got us to India sooner. India teased, and India was where I wanted to be. A sleepover was all I needed to satisfy me in my time spent in Pakistan.

Chapter 10

India held the greatest fascination and allure for me, so much so I placed it in the crevices of my mind relating to the Milky Way or time-space dimensions, something real yet surreal.

Then suddenly it dawned on me, after I left Lahore, I was really going to India. Right now. It had never seemed possible before.

I'd felt that way about Israel, but only after I got there. I was so obsessed with getting to Israel to help the war effort that, once there, I realized where I was and all it meant to me. But even then, Israel was my surreal place, a place special for me as a Jew, and real enough that I did have at least some notion I would get there someday.

But with India, after all the books I had read, the philosophies coming from there for millennia, the sciences, the religions, the crown jewel of an empire so vast that the sun never set, it seemed more fairy tale to me than fact, somehow, in my spiritual reverence for it.

I hated the way India struggled these days, however. I didn't blame the British for that so much, in spite of some detrimental divide-and-conquer policies they'd used. I blamed socialism. But India's problems began before socialism or the British. These philosophies and religions that I loved from India were also partially to blame for their current problems. India got bogged down by the weight of its own brilliant inertia. It began to stagnate even though opportunities for change were presented. The caste system, being the worst element of their cultural inertia, enslaved their society and left them vulnerable to conqueror after conqueror.

But even then, the way India gained their independence from the British through *satyagraha*, or peaceful resistance, was as brilliant and progressive as it was courageous. And it exerted all the power their cultural and spiritual DNA still maintained.

We entered India at Amritsar in the Punjab, just across from Lahore in Pakistan. As poor as India was, it was the India worth coming overland to see. Almost immediately, even before finding a hotel, Ewa and I made our way to the Sikh Golden Temple, just to know we saw it, just for that first impact.

It was ironic to start off with a minority segment of the country. India was Hindu, although it had one of the largest Muslim populations in the world. Buddhism began in ancient India. And here we were starting our India quest at the center of Sikhism. The Sikhs only originated in the fifteenth century, right at the time of Columbus discovering the new world. And compared with the other major religions in India, it was one of the smallest, only twenty million Sikhs, whereas the Hindus approached a billion people. But that twenty-million Sikh population was almost half again the entire Jewish population in the world. That didn't get lost on me.

"Oh, Hunter!" Ewa swooned as we approached the grounds of the Golden Temple. "How beautiful it is. It is like it really is made of gold."

"And it's built in the middle of this water pond."

"Hunter, I am so tired, and we have our backpacks. Let us find a place nearby. Or near enough. I just wanted to see the Temple first, to rejuvenate me after two weeks of struggle getting here. But I want to do it justice. Is that how you express giving time and devotion to a place? To do it justice? So we will find a place, take a rest break, and come back here to walk around and have someone explain about the Sihks and the Temple. We can go inside then."

I nodded approval at her idea as I kept staring, mesmerized by the Temple in front of us.

But immediately, the poverty overwhelmed us the farther we walked away from the Temple area. Beggars, filth from garbage and trash disposal, human excrement, animal waste, and just plain smog and grime was everywhere. Plus, India, like Pakistan, was densely overcrowded. All the more reason to want to return to the Temple later. To rejuvenate once again, as well as know there is glory in India.

At least our hostel was clean. We got a nice-sized room with a double bed in a hostel less than a half hour's walk from the Golden Temple. The springs inside the mattress were a bit squeaky, but there was enough padding that our rest would be unimpaired.

"I am sweating some," Ewa commented as we checked into our room.

"It's been warm since we got past the Khyber Pass," I said happily. "Like spring weather back home in Texas. I can start going around in T-shirts now."

"Do you have any shirts like T-shirt?" she asked.

"A couple. I'll buy some more here someplace."

"I must also. But we should wait. I want to see the

different clothing in the markets."

"I'm glad they don't have an attached bathroom in this place," I said displaying a serious look on my face.

"Why? We were given again a bucket for our bath. Same as in Lahore. I do not remember anymore in my mind what is a shower or now even a real bath."

"But I'm telling you. It's good we don't have a bathroom attached."

I began a brisk walk to the door.

"Aha," Ewa said, showing concern. "I think you must have diarrhea, then, Hunter."

I nodded yes as I rushed on down the hall to the men's bathroom. Thank God no one was using it.

By the time I got back to our room, Ewa had not only unpacked her belongings but also mine. She looked up from the bed when I reentered.

"Are you all right, Hunter?"

"I've heard some real bad stories about diarrhea and India. I hope I don't have too many to add to it. I'm sure I got some bad creatures in my gut at Lahore. At that market we ate in, the kid served me garbanzo beans from a rusty coffee can and with a rusty spoon. I was hoping they were at least clean, but even then, I thought, you know, I might as well start getting my antibodies now. Well, something is growing and growling in my belly. I hope some of them are winning the war being fought with the bad bacteria."

"I do not have bad bowels yet, diarrhea, but I also experience some problems already. Yes, maybe it is good we do not have attached bathrooms now."

As soon as we were rested, we walked back to the Golden Temple. It was so uplifting to see even from a distance.

A young bearded, turbaned man approached us as we entered the Temple area. All Sikh men wear turbans wrapped around their heads. Under the turbans are a lifelong growth of hair, as they are not allowed to cut their hair or their beards.

"I can show you our Temple and explain, if you like," the young man offered.

Ewa and I looked at one another and agreed to allow him. We had to watch our money, but he was impoverished and knowledgeable. The price he charged was theoretically free, but even if we were generous, it would amount to a small payment in the exchange rate.

"The Temple," our guide explained as we walked toward the Temple itself, "was completed early in the seventeenth century."

He was silent as we approached the entrance. We could already hear organ music. It held a rhythmic, almost hypnotic sway, similar to music we'd heard in our previously visited Asian countries.

"When Islamic rulers conquered India," he continued as he stood facing us while he talked just beyond the doors of the entrance, "many changes began to occur in India. India has been conquered many times, but no conqueror made an impact as did the Mughal rulers. Islam is still very prominent in our midst even today. Many of the untouchables in our caste system, the lowest class of the masses, joined Islam. With their new religion and their new class and freedom, many became very militant."

Ewa and I stood intently looking at him as he spoke. He seemed to enjoy educating us.

"Through the centuries of Mughal rule, the concept of one God became more acceptable in India even among the Hindu. The Hindu religion is very tolerant of other religions. Hindus have many gods, but accept other religions' gods also in some way. But eventually, other untouchables and other castes began to accept strongly the idea of one God. But still they hated the Islamic rulers. That is when Sikhism began, and by the eighteenth century it was well established. There was much suppression of our religion, and many of the Mughal rulers martyred many of our gurus. But we became strong by the eighteenth century."

"You have problems even now, right?" I asked him.

"Oh, yes. We wish to form our own country, much like the Muslims did with Pakistan. Earlier this year, there was a large conflict about this. There are laws of discrimination against us, and many Sikhs want to break away. We had a peaceful demonstration earlier this year, and many of us were martyred."

"You believe in one God?" Ewa asked in amazement. "Is it the Jewish or Islamic God?"

"There are differences," he said. "Of course there is but one God, but we do not always have the same idea about it."

We waited for an explanation.

"We can claim we worship the same one God, but since we have different holy scriptures, dress, and customs, we are a separate people. Many of our beliefs in justice, family, and helping others are much the same. But following different scriptures is the main difference, and you can determine if we all follow the same God."

Ewa and I looked at one another. Was he sliding by on his explanation for convenience or politeness? I had to assume the Sikhs were influenced by both Islam and Hinduism in their philosophies and outlooks.

Our guide explained the Temple itself, with its decorative gildings and marble. The ceiling looked similar to mosaic to me, though the walls and ceiling contained some gold. All this contrasted with the poverty surrounding the Temple. Somehow it made the place all the more a refuge and sacred to its followers. Even poor people had a place to go to uplift themselves. If all the wealth of the Temple were stripped and distributed, there would be nothing to show for it after a few days, but the Temple as it stood was long-lasting.

Our first night in India! This was an accomplishment. Not only because India was special in world history, but because it was a jewel now, to my generation. The poverty around me was overwhelming, and the filth unimaginable. But it was still India.

"India is a vegetarian country," Ewa commented. "Muslims eat meat. I guess that means we can have meat at least sometimes here."

"The Sikh religion allows meat," I commented. "That means, for us, we better get it while we can. I've always wondered how true vegetarians do it. Their diet, I mean. When I was growing up in Texas, steak-and-potatoes country, I remember when I first heard about vegetarians. So I pictured our diet but without meat—sounded horrible and boring. Somehow it's not. They know what to do here about diets and recipes and protein. So we'll see. But tonight, let's indulge in meat for one last time."

Everywhere we walked were turbaned men, their long hair under the turbans and long beards pulled up and wrapped inside it as well. If that's all one knows, I decided, it must work out. But I couldn't fathom putting up with all that hair.

"These men without turbans," Ewa mentioned curiously. "I wonder if they are Hindu or Muslim. Or do a certain percentage of Sihks also secularize enough to not bother with turbans?"

After seeing the filthy streets all around us, our room looked especially clean.

"Where do we go next?" Ewa asked me as we lay in bed the next morning. "Where is this place we are going?"

"We're headed to Baroda. But that's a ways away yet. Where we're going first this morning is Delhi, to see the Red Fort. We should get there by this afternoon."

"Delhi to see the Red Fort," Ewa repeated, as if to formalize it in her mind. "When must we arrive in Baroda?"

"No set time to get there. They just know we're on our way. Any day now."

But I was anxious to get there. I intended to see only the spotlight sites along the way, so much so I was bypassing the sacred Ganges River. It was close enough, perhaps a couple of hours farther east from New Delhi, but I allowed myself to believe I would get to it somewhere after my stay in Baroda.

Chapter 11

We had to elbow our way to get on the train. The first class cars were expensive, and taking one of those would be copping out, it seemed to me. I wanted the jungle-class cars; I wanted the every-man-for-himself accommodation. And that's exactly what we got.

Massive numbers of bodies crammed onto the cars in the non-reserved portions of the train. Being tall, being white-skinned, being a foreigner, and not being used to gang warfare made me shy to fight my way for a seat—or even for a sliver of space for standing. Ewa followed me as if I were a fullback in a football game blocking interference for the ball carrier. She even grabbed the back of my belted trousers and hung on for dear life.

I noticed more and more of the masses crawling out the windows, grabbing hold of the guardrails at the top of the cars on the outside and pulling themselves up to ride on top of the train. That looked like fun. If I was going to be miserable, fun was the way to do it.

"Let me go first," I said to Ewa as I studied the window space on how I was to exit without getting killed.

"Go first where, Hunter?"

"Come to my side now, Ewa. We're going on top."

"On top of where?" she asked as she peered from behind me to see. "Hunter, no!" she gasped as she saw the objective before us.

"Look at these people, Ewa. Watch how they climb out of the window holding on to the ridge. See how they plant their feet on the window ledge, grab hold of the steel bars on top of the train, and pull themselves up. Even women smaller than you are doing this. We can manage."

She looked up at me skeptically, then grimaced as if game.

"What about our backpacks?" she asked, still showing concern.

"They're small. Let me go first. I'll take yours after I'm up, then help pull you up."

"Don't fall," she cautioned.

"The train is moving slowly. We'll be okay. We can manage this."

The smiles on the faces of the Indian travelers already on top of the train encouraged me. They graciously made room for me and even pulled on my shoulders, trying to help me up. I nodded my thanks to them as I twisted and turned to find a secure place on top. I followed their lead by placing my feet firmly against the steel bar with my legs and seat area squarely on the top frame.

Once confident I was stable, I pulled off my backpack and placed it between myself and the man on the other side of the top from me. I leaned back, turned on my belly, then twisted a hundred eighty degrees, ending head down, in order to face Ewa at the window to help her up. First, I grabbed her backpack and secured it next to mine, then grabbed one of her wrists and gripped it tightly to give her confidence. Once she began to crawl out of the window, I pulled her toward me. As she reached the top, I grabbed her with both arms under her shoulders and drew her up next to me.

"Ho," she huffed out with a laugh. "I will never forgive you if we are killed."

"Look at the view, though, Ewa. All this jungle around us is ours. We're the masters."

She nodded approvingly.

Halfway to Delhi, we had to disembark to take a bus. I was ready for a change because riding without seat support can strain muscles.

"You are here for the ashram?" A man asked us as we sat at a restaurant we found in our new town.

"What ashram?" I asked.

"Rishikesh?" Ewa asked curiously.

"Oh, no," the man remarked. "Rishikesh is far from here, two, maybe three hours to the east of here. Are you from Europe?"

"America," I answered.

"That is very well. You do not need to go to Rishikesh. Too many people there. And the Maharishi Mahesh Yogi is not there many times. So many from Europe, and some from America, find other ashrams just as well. Do you come for the ashram here? It is not far."

I looked at Ewa inquisitively.

"Would you like to see an ashram?" I asked her.

She shook her head. "It makes to me no difference."

"We're here. I would like to see some of this stuff."

"I thought we were going to live on one in Baroda," Ewa commented.

"Yeah, but again, the people in Baroda are social

workers. I prefer that. It seems authentic to me. They are social workers first and Hindus second. But all this ashram stuff that people flock here for ever since the Beatles, that could be interesting, too, even if it's hype, so let's check this local one out."

Ewa once again shook her head indifferently. "I am with you. We have good experiences together. I am amenable to your ideas and wishes, Hunter. We can visit this ashram if you like."

"There are many like you," the man talking with us said, "so many from Europe wanting to talk to swamis and *sadhus* to understand philosophy and thinking. It is good for our town. You are very welcome here. I can show you the bus to get to the ashram. But it is not so far. Take a taxi is better. I can show you a taxi and help you to get there. But do not let the taxi cheat you. They cheat Americans."

Taking what the man called a taxi was also an experience, even though we had the taxi to ourselves. It was a motorcycle taxi but with three wheels, one at the front for steering, and two at the rear on each side of compartments that held two seats for passengers. A motored rickshaw. Our driver wore a turban, though not the bulky type we saw Sikhs wearing in the Punjab. His clothing was much like that of the man we met in town, ragged and dirty.

"You are American?" The rickshaw driver asked us at the entrance to the ashram.

I nodded.

"Good. I am very poor."

What did that mean, I wondered? I found out. He charged us just for being rich Americans. I refused to pay it.

"But I am very poor, sir."

"So am I," I countered.

"Americans are very rich. You must pay more."

"But I'm not going to pay more."

I handed him what I considered a fair price.

"You must pay more," the man said. "Other drivers will also charge you more."

"I'd rather they have my money than you. How's that? I ain't going to pay more."

The driver looked at me angrily but took my small payment and drove away.

Before we got to a building in front of us, two American-looking men and three American-looking women walked over to us. They had been working in a garden near the building. The two men had hair just above their shoulders and were bearded. They wore robe-like garments that extended to their knees. The women all had hair past their shoulders and wore robe-like dresses that went almost to their ankles.

"Where are you from?" One of the two men asked me in an American accent.

"Texas."

"Yippee," he mocked with a chuckle. "We're all Americans. The five of us here, I mean."

I smiled politely.

"Did you come to join our ashram?" he asked, transforming into a serious demeanor.

"No, we're on our way to Baroda. We have some friends there. Someone told us about you, though, and we were in the area, so we thought we'd come by and check things out."

"It's very good here," said the tallest girl. "Our guru is very wise. We learn a great deal from him."

I nodded polite approval.

A turbaned Indian man with a beard came out of the nearby building and made his way to us. The five Americans smiled his way as he did so.

"*Namaste*," he greeted with a smile as he held his hands in a prayerful gesture.

"It is nice to meet you," Ewa returned.

"Whoa," the first of the Americans I'd talked to said. "You're not American."

"I come from Poland."

"Wow," all five said in unison. "Welcome."

"Thank you."

"So what's it like here?" I asked.

"It's so good to get out of the rat race," the tall girl said, "away from materialism."

I could identify with that. Maybe.

"What got you here, though?" I asked pointedly.

"I was sick of my job," the first man said. "I was missing something. Everyone had heard of the Mahesh Yogi, but I read about this place in a magazine article once."

"Same here," another of the girls said. "I was a secretary in Toledo. I came across an article about things happening in India. After I got here, someone in Delhi, in a hostel I was at, told me about this place."

"What do you do while you're here?"

"We meditate," the tall girl said. "We work in the garden. We talk with our guru. We study."

With that, all five looked at the turbaned Indian, who once again smiled my way.

"Peace can be found," the guru said, "inside one's innermost self. Turn away the world and simply find yourself inside."

"You can do that in Toledo," I said.

"No," the girl from Toledo said pointedly. "Too many distractions. Too much pollution."

"What about all the poverty here?" I asked. "Isn't that distracting?"

"Only to those bogged down in the material world," the first American said. "Jesus faced many of these same elements in his day. What he offered was the kingdom of God. Inner peace. Oneness with the universe."

"Do you hope to find what you need here and be better equipped for when you go back home?" I asked.

"We will know when that occurs," the tall girl answered. "Our guru guides us daily."

"Would you like something to eat?" The first man asked.

"You must worry about your health," the tall girl said. "Eat well and gain nourishment. This is a part of inner peace and harmony."

"We just ate something in town," Ewa said.

"Would you like to stay for the night?" The tall girl asked.

"We are expected at our ashram in Baroda," I said.

"Oh, it's an ashram you're going to in Baroda," the first man said. "Very good."

"Yes," I replied. "We're on our way, and they expect us by tomorrow," I lied. "We were just curious what all is happening here. So many Westerners come here."

"There is much dissatisfaction in the industrialized countries," the tall girl said. "The more we look to possessions for our happiness, the more we get bogged down with materialism."

"Good luck," I replied.

All five wore broad, exaggerated smiles. The guru smiled while bowing his head and putting his hands in a prayerful manner again.

"Good-bye," Ewa said as we walked back toward the road to look for a taxi.

Neither one of us said anything until we got to the highway. Then Ewa looked at me.

"Is this why we go to Baroda?" she asked sourly.

I shook my head no. "But this is exactly why I came to India," I replied. "I want to check out what's going on here. I have my own agenda too. But I came also for the adventure of it all. I had the feeling this was going on. Packaged enlightenment."

"They seemed so phony, Hunter. I am not trying to show disrespect, but I could not believe they were trying to be serious."

"They are probably getting something good out of it. Maybe they'll filter out any of the phony hype. Where we're going are social workers, like I told you. I do want to check out the phonies, if that's what they are, but I'm looking for authenticity. I'm not looking to find my head here. I want to experience some things. Even phony stuff. I want to see what all the hubbub is about and make up my own mind. There are phonies back home, too, in churches. And I know there are real people here who get things out of Hinduism and Eastern thought. Since they are religious where we're going, and not trying to proselytize, that sounds perfect. We'll see religion in their works and hear what they've got to say. I remember the Beatles started off wanting the spiritual from here. They went to Rishikesh and were very turned off real quick. They all went home early. John Lennon ended up writing that song *Sexy Sadie* about it all. Coded sarcasm, you know."

"Maybe we do not understand, Hunter. Maybe coming here helps these people and we do not understand and so it seems phony to us."

"You never know," I said with a sigh. "But looking at it, it just seems like another denomination of a cult. Enlightenment, Inc."

I looked at her and smirked.

"At least we can mark Rishikesh off the list to go see," I commented. "So onward to the Red Fort. We can still make it to Delhi today, and we'll check it out first thing in the morning."

Chapter 12

If we had flown directly to Delhi from Vienna, we might have been overwhelmed upon our arrival. Already the overcrowding, the poverty, and the filth had to be dealt with, but the overland adventure had helped prepare us by the time we got there, and even inoculated us. Delhi included all we'd experienced about India up to then, but in geometric proportions far greater. It got to me, but amazingly I could handle it. My psychological antibodies were up to the task of enjoying Delhi in spite of the poverty and filth on the streets.

Just to be in the former capital innervated me, but all the more because the Red Fort was there. The Red Fort was the main residence of the emperors of the Mughal dynasty for nearly two hundred years, until 1857.

The Hindu religion, which dominated India for millennia, is very passive. It breeds, in its philosophy and mindset, nonviolence. Hence, Mahatma Gandhi's satyagraha, or peaceful resistance revolution, that spurred the removal of the British. India, in fact, has been conquered many times. But until the Mughal invasion, the conquering country was more conquered by their subjects in India than dominating like a conqueror should be.

But the Mughals made a major impact. They were

Muslim, and now almost fifteen percent of India is Muslim, plus most of the populations of Pakistan and Bangladesh, which were then part of India. Islam was originally introduced into India much like in other countries, through contact with traders. Turkish groups also invaded parts of India to make an impact.

Hinduism was challenged and diminished by the Mughals, though it still remains the dominant religion and philosophy. Where Hinduism had weaknesses, as in its caste system, especially with the untouchables, conversion to Islam often appealed to the oppressed and succeeded abundantly. Islam looked strong and, to many, more just.

The Red Fort and its museums, on the Yamuna River, are the symbols of this Islamic strength and appeal. Its architecture is beautiful in typical Muslim fashion and spreads over two square miles surrounded by defensive walls. It is punctuated by turrets and bastions. There are marble floral-decorated double domes in the fort's buildings. The fort's artwork blends Persian, European, and Indian art, resulting in a unique style rich in form, expression, and color.

Ewa and I spent most of the next day trying to take in at least portions of every facet of the fort, including some of its museums. The rest of Delhi and even nearby New Delhi, the current Indian capital, had little appeal to us. We had too much of India to experience to consider these massive cities for now. Agra, the capital before Delhi, was the site of the Taj Mahal, one of the wonders of the world, which demanded our immediate attention next. Our bus got us there just before nightfall.

"Should we go see the Taj Mahal before we find a hotel?" Ewa asked.

"How do you feel?" I asked her.

"I am very tired, in fact, after all the travelling on overcrowded buses and after walking for hours at this Red Fort complex. But we are here, and we could see the Taj Mahal all lit up like in pictures. Is it worth it to you for that?"

"Almost. But I'll settle for a hotel or a hostel. Whatever we find soon. I'd rather see the Taj Mahal rested."

"I am very glad you said this opinion. That is how I feel. And I tell you, for what energy I have remaining, the longer we are on the streets, the more we are swarmed by the beggars. I know we must look like rich tourists. I see how poor everyone is, and I know they are desperate. But we have limited money, and we are half way around the world with so little money. And when we give money, even a small amount, we are swarmed even more. I know I do not have energy to see the Taj Mahal and deal with all the beggars that are everywhere."

I wanted to give my take on the beggars, since she brought it up, but I wasn't sure just what my take on them was. When I was a boy in South Texas, we came upon many beggars when we visited Mexico. Nothing had prepared me for what we faced in India, however. Human reactions to it, positive and negative, flooded me. I could handle only so much emotionally from the horror and pity I felt, or for the disdain and frustration from being bombarded constantly.

Plus, new elements hit us since we left the Punjab, as we walked the streets of India. For all the trash, garbage, and human excrement everywhere, there was now even more excrement to face in the remainder of

India. Hindus are over eighty percent of the population. They are vegetarians. That should mean there are no animals to raise for slaughter. Thus, no livestock to deal with. But there was livestock everywhere. The Brahma breed of cattle is a godlike creature to the Hindus. These beasts are allowed to roam the streets at will. And excrete. Even on the river banks, human and animal waste was abundant. Roaches and rats were also abundant, to feast on it all.

We found a hostel close enough to the Taj Mahal yet far enough away to allow a reasonable price.

"We should get something to eat before we take our bucket shower," Ewa suggested. "We will get hot and sweaty again if we wait to eat afterwards, or step in the filth on the street."

I nodded agreement. We threw our backpacks onto our bed and ventured back out into the streets.

"You know," I said to Ewa with a grin on my face as we sat at our restaurant table. "I could be a vegetarian. They know what they are doing here. I shouldn't be shocked, but I am. I don't miss meat anymore, since the food is so good—the spices, the flavors, and texture."

"With an egg or milk, we are fine with our animal protein," she replied.

"And you know," I mused further, "back home we are semi-tropical in our climate, which means it's hot for most of the year, which means you have to have the right kind of livestock. There are ticks and other parasites. Also, northern breeds of cattle don't always do well in South Texas heat. So among the breeds we imported was Brahma cattle."

"Like here in India."

"From here, I'm sure. I heard that, anyway. But here's the point. We have rodeos. I don't know if you've heard of them. But cowboys ride bucking broncos and bulls. Mostly Brahma bulls. They are the meanest creatures alive. It's like they have a switchblade. I mean, they hate your everloving guts. Not just the ones in a rodeo, but on our farms and ranches, too. If you're in a pasture with any Brahmas— we call them bramers—you better have your last will and testament made out, because if you ain't paying attention, you just might wake up dead. Some breeds of cattle simply try to bust the fence down to escape. Brahmas take being penned up and branded very personal, though. Meaning *you*. They *hate* you. Hate. Stomping, snorting hate."

"But they are so gentle on the streets here," Ewa said. "I am not at all afraid to pet them. They walk up to you as if you are their best friend in the whole world."

"Yeah, that's exactly right, and why I brought it up. They seem to respond differently to people that eat them than to those that treat them as a god."

"You are funny, my dear man, but I like that. I like what you say. You are such an observer. A philosopher, even. I can say observations about my home also. The way the politburo treats the proletariat and the same result that comes from a bull being eaten."

****

I had seen pictures of the Taj Mahal a thousand times or more. But to see its magnificence in person was breathtaking. The name itself means Crown of the Palace. Ewa and I could not talk. We held hands and stared.

"It is a tomb," Ewa said to break the silence. "A

mausoleum. Is that not precious? This Mughal Shah was grief-stricken over the death of his wife, his favorite wife, and he builds a wonder of the world to her memory, a memory of love and devotion. I am so moved, Hunter, beyond words. To be so loved—we can only dream of such love."

"She died giving birth," I added.

"Oh, my God, it breaks my heart. Hunter, I am almost in tears to think of such tragedy and such love. I cannot get past the love devotion. Am I too sentimental?"

"Tagore, the poet, called the Taj Mahal a teardrop on the cheek of time."

She squeezed my hand all the more.

The emotion we felt was too strong to worry what others thought of us. We held hands the entire time we walked portions of the complex's forty-two acres. To express love emotions was to pay homage as much as to try to absorb all the majesty we saw before us. We walked alongside the reflecting pool, the marble-domed structure itself, through the gardens, along the red sandstone outer walls, and on to the red sandstone mosque.

This is all we wanted from Agra, even though it also had been a capital of India. I wished to remember nothing more of the city than its grandest edifice.

"India will make a comeback," I said sympathetically that night as Ewa and I lay in bed. "It is too great a civilization not to. It has given too much to the world to not receive its own grandeur. It doesn't know how to fail. It's only cleansing itself of impurities."

She stroked my cheek in support of what I said.

"Where next, Hunter?"

"I'm anxious to go on to Baroda now. Baroda is almost due south of here. I'm not sure we can get there tomorrow. It depends on our luck with the trains. It's several hundred miles from here. We'll probably make a stop for the night before we get there. I can't think of what to see on the way, so we'll just go until we're tired, and then continue the next day."

I looked at her to celebrate the thought.

"Once we're in Baroda, we can unpack and unwind," I said. "Just live."

"How long will we stay in Baroda?" she asked.

"I don't know. We'll just see what's going on and play it day by day. When do you have to be back in Vienna?"

"I am like you for now. I am so much into my life for now, this is all I can think of."

"But what about your father? What's he think of all this?"

"I was ready to start a term in music school soon. I left a message to him through the Polish Embassy that I will miss the next session, that I have an address in India and want to take advantage of the opportunity."

"That's it? You said that and he's supposed to not have a heart attack? He may pull you out of school."

She nodded her head as if it was a possibility.

"You know," I said with a sigh, "we were in New Delhi, the capital, just yesterday. I should have taken you to the Polish Embassy. I didn't think about it because you seemed to know what you were doing. But there may be a message for you there from him. You may be in serious trouble. I'm glad you're here with me, but it may have gotten you into trouble big-time.

He may pull you back to Warsaw and never again let you out of his politburo sight."

She let out a chuckle.

"My father is not that important. He is not with the politburo. Not the powers of it."

"He's powerful enough, and you may have abused it."

She nodded again. This was worrying me now.

"That is why I do not want to go to the embassy," she commented. "I do not want such a message. Especially now while I am still with you. I will go soon enough. And if I can never leave Warsaw again, at least I did this." She stared at me and rubbed my cheek. "At least I met you. I will worry about the rest when it happens. Please, Hunter, let us complete our fate together before we worry about such things."

Chapter 13

As excited as I was to get to my first makeshift home in India, I was suddenly feeling anxiety over losing Ewa in my life. How was I going to work all of this? Why didn't I get to be happy about soon reaching my destination? Instead, haunting visions absorbed me at just the thought of losing the love of my life once I did arrive in Baroda. I didn't know her father, and I certainly didn't understand her relationship with him, much less the setting in which she was living in her Polish world. I was so comfortable with Ewa in my life now, and she was such a deep part of me. So I had all this anxiety inside me, horrible anxiety.

I had been so happy because of her, until these fears of losing her came along. Every day had been the most important day in my life because it was a day I had with her. But now the days would have an uncertain future.

I couldn't put these fears out of my mind, but I was determined not to let them ruin my time while I was still with her. We would deal with what we had to. I soon focused once again on the journey to Baroda.

Ewa and I immediately went for the roof of the train on our last stretch to Baroda. It was fun, and you met the nicest people there.

"Are you a *sannyasi*?" I asked the man sitting next to me on top of the train.

"Yes. You know what this is, to be a sannyasi?"

"I see your orange robe to your knees. I've seen pictures of Buddhist monks wearing saffron robes. I just made a stab at what you are, since we're in India, guessing you've renounced everything to follow a life of detachment and asceticism within Hindu philosophy."

He smiled at me.

"You sound like a professor. But yes, this is true. I am in the beginning stage, however. It is called the level of *Brahmacharya*. A true sannyasi is for the later years in life, the years of reflection. But I am not so much a brahmachari, because I have not remained with a teacher as a student. I am young and in the student stage, but I wander. I have many teachers."

I saw the puzzled look on Ewa's face as she listened to his explanation.

"Would you enjoy some of my, uh, what do you call these?" Ewa asked him while trying to offer some of her snacks that we'd bought just before we boarded the train to Baroda.

"*Chivda*," the brahmachari replied. "This type of chivda is made from dried lentil beans."

She held out her cup for him to take from it, and flinched when he grabbed half of the contents of her cup. This happened to us a great deal. The sannyasis, or brahmacharis, were the worst, in fact. So much for asceticism and denunciation. Since we were foreigners and technically rich, I had to assume the gods weren't looking just now. Or so he seemed to think.

It was hot, and we were sun-blistered by the time we arrived at Baroda, even with the suntans we'd already developed from previous days. Our tans made our new sunburns somewhat bearable, at least.

"Bargain for the price beforehand," Ewa suggested as we flagged down a motor rickshaw to take us to our ashram.

"Can you take us here?" I asked the driver while showing him my address book.

"Oh, yes, for certain, sir. Yes, please get in. I take you immediately there."

I handed him the money and waited for his response.

"Oh, no, sir, I am sorry. I need so much more money. Please, sir, you are American. You must understand my situation here."

"I understand you probably want to overcharge me because you think I am rich."

"Oh, but kind sir, all the taxis here will charge you more."

"I'd rather they have my money than you, then. Take it or leave it."

The driver looked at me in disbelief, then reluctantly nodded his head for us to get in.

Baroda was one of the larger cities in the state of Gujurat. I had never heard of Baroda itself until my friend gave me the address of the ashram where we were going to stay. But I had heard of Gujurat, since it was the Indian state of Mahatma Gandhi's origin.

I had no expectations, really, as we approached the ashram, except that the swami running the place was not a hustler of Western cultic airheads. He was supposedly a legitimate religious swami, not caring if I wanted to be Hindu or not. I wanted to see daily life here, and since they were social workers first, I was looking forward to my stay with them. In fact, Swami

Subbaraya was the only religious Brahmin in this ashram. The rest were secular, though of a religious nature. Perfect. I wanted to be exposed to the Hindu religion but not pressured into it. I mostly wanted a normal life to relate to while I was here.

The ashram was on the edge of town and enclosed by a large concrete wall with peeling maroon paint. It had a thick wooden door at the front. I began to pound on it to get attention.

An elderly man with specks of gray hair opened the door. He looked at me curiously, then eased into a smile.

"May I help you, please?" he asked.

"I hope so," I replied. "I'm looking for Sri Achyut."

"That is my brother. May I help you? I am Sri Sitaram. This is the ashram for Swamiji Subbaraya. You seem to be American. Are you the one from Texas we are expecting since a month ago now? Are you Hunter? Hunter from Texas? Is this your name, please?"

"Yes, great, yeah, sure." I held out my hand enthusiastically. "I'm Hunter. A friend of Jim's." I turned toward Ewa. "And this is my friend Ewa."

Sri Sitaram looked her way and smiled, bowed slightly, and brought his hands up to a prayerful position.

"We were not expecting a young lady," he said.

"Is it okay? We came from Vienna. She's my friend, not Jim's, so he didn't know to mention her."

"That is no problem. She is very welcomed."

"I should have mentioned her in my letter to you before I left Texas," I lied, "but I wasn't for sure yet if she could make it or not."

"Yes, of course, we are happy to have her. Please, won't you come in? We have many rooms set up for guests."

Rooms. Plural. As in one for each of us. I had expected as much but hoped for better.

"Should I show him our marriage certificate?" Ewa whispered as we followed Sri Sitaram into the complex.

I shook my head no.

"We have to play the game now," I cautioned her.

She gave a polite smile of understanding the situation, but then purposely huffed a deflated sigh of disappointment.

Sri Sitaram turned back to us for a moment as we walked.

"You certainly are a strong young man," he said with a laugh. "I thought someone had a battering ram at the door. I was surprised to see only one man as responsible for the barrage."

"I just saw your wall. I thought maybe y'all were off in a building somewhere and couldn't hear."

"We most certainly heard you."

He led us to a building just to the side of the entrance door. There, two other men and a woman were seated at a table, eating papaya and sipping tea.

"This is Sri Achyut," Sri Sitaram explained, pointing to a man at the table.

An elderly man with a full head of gray hair turned to us and smiled. "Is this the one from Texas we have been expecting?"

"This is Hunter," Sri Sitaram said. He then turned toward Ewa. "And this is his friend from Vienna, named Ewa."

119

"Very nice," Sri Achyut replied. "Won't you share some *chai* with us? Chai is what we call tea. It is the middle of the afternoon. We are expecting a man from a society that will provide dentists for us tomorrow. You are in luck. We will go to a nearby village where there are many people with dental problems. Several dentists from Baroda will accompany us tomorrow and provide free care throughout the day. We will all go in a van provided by the society. You will get to see a rural Indian village, but also you will see among the poorest in India."

"Have a seat," Sri Sitaram said as he motioned Ewa and me to chairs at the table with the others. "If you prefer coffee, Hunter, we can provide for you. Also you, Ewa. Anything you would like. Then we will show you to your rooms. Hunter, if it is good with you, you will stay in a room with a brahmachari from Nigeria. Ewa, there is a room with one of our servant girls in the building next to it."

"That is so considerate of you, Sri Sitaram," Ewa said nervously. "But may I ask… May I please stay in the same building as my friend Hunter? I understand the appropriateness of such separation, but we have been through so much in the overland journey here. We are quite used to one another. I would like it to be convenient to visit him easily and often. We may have to split up after we leave the ashram, since I am from Poland. You know the complexity there."

"Poland?" Sri Achyut gasped. "You are from Poland and have been travelling freely with an American over Asia?"

"Yes, that is true. It is very difficult circumstances, as you can imagine. We will be quite honorable and show all needed protocol and respect. But we would like to be able to feel free, with certain limits, of course, to be near one another and share our remaining private time together. Except for sleeping, of course."

Sri Sitaram and Sri Achyut looked at one another for a moment, then said something in dialect. They then nodded at one another and turned back to Ewa.

"Yes, of course," Sri Achyut replied. "Poland. I am anxious to hear your story, how you arranged such a journey under these circumstances, especially with an American. There is a room in the building with Hunter and Brahmachari. That is what we call him, Brahmachari. He is an initiate, a devotee, whose real name is George. While he is here, we simply call him by his title. The room with them is attached to your room. You will have your own toilet and bath. You will have your privacy, but it is attached to their room. We trust you to show manners. It is quite all right."

A servant girl brought out two more cups of tea and a fresh plate of papayas with a knife to cut them into slices.

"Tea is fine for me, Sri Sitaram," I said, "but if you do have coffee, I would prefer it in the future, if you don't mind."

"As you wish."

Ewa and I stayed during the tea break until the people from the dental society arrived to arrange the next day's charitable service. A servant girl then led us to our rooms where we would be staying during our time at the ashram.

The girl tapped on the door in a nearby building. There was no answer, so she opened the door slightly and peeked in.

"Brahmachari is in meditation now," she explained just above a whisper. "Come, we will not disturb him. But we must be quiet, for courtesy."

She opened the door completely and motioned for us to follow her. On the floor against the wall toward the back of the room was a black man sitting in lotus position with his eyes closed. His head was completely shaven, and he wore a yellow robe. She led us past him to an adjacent room that would be for Ewa.

"Can you leave us here?" I asked the servant girl. "We don't want to disturb Brahmachari. As soon as he awakens, I'll leave this room. Is that all right?"

The girl looked unsure of herself but then nodded approval and left us to ourselves.

As soon as the girl closed the door behind her, Ewa leaned forcefully into my side with her head and upper body. I put my arm around her as she embraced me.

"I will behave myself, Hunter, but it will be agony. Pure agony. I will do this from respect, but somewhere every day we will have to find a place where I can kiss you. I will not go even one day without a kiss from you. I mean a deep kiss. Like this."

She then raised her head up, pulled at my neck, and kissed me forcefully and desperately.

"Welcome to Baroda, Hunter. Welcome to the ashram. I will not make love to you while we are here, but I will want to do this glorious undertaking. Every day I will want you. Do you understand this from me, Hunter? But I demand my kiss. I will and must have my embrace and kiss from you every single day."

I kissed her on my own as if to seal the vow.

Chapter 14

"So, how are your accommodations?" Sri Achyut asked Ewa and me in the van on our way to the dental clinic the next morning.

"They were very nice," Ewa praised. "Everything is so clean. And I am so grateful to you for allowing Hunter and me to have adjacent rooms together. I hope you did not break any rules on our behalf."

"Everything is fine," Sri Sitaram answered with a smile. "I am glad you understand our customs require a certain protocol. We are a charitable organization and we cannot afford to have any improprieties. We do not want anyone to lose confidence in us. But I think everyone is fine with separate rooms even if adjacent. An exception can be made here."

"What is really happening," Brahmachari said, with a grin, in his strong African accent, "is they take the religious part of their ashram very seriously also."

Everyone waited for an explanation.

"I am an initiate," Brahmachari continued. "I must abstain from worldly pleasures and temptations. To make sure I am focused, Sri Achyut and Sri Sitaram have arranged the ultimate in temptation for me. A true test of my skills in denunciation. To place this goddess in the room right next to me is the ultimate in focus and strengthening. You must thank Swamiji for his confidence in me."

Everyone laughed.

Brahmachari was very down to earth. We enjoyed each other right from the beginning, following his meditation the previous day. I wasn't surprised, but my experiences and observations had seen the more naïve aspects of devotees. To see an authentic ashram in its natural state was refreshing to me and reassured me that coming here was the right thing to do.

"Do you understand what a swami is?" Sri Achyut asked. "And do you understand the suffix that Brahmachari used—the 'ji' at the end of 'swami'—'swamiji'? That is a sign of affection and respect. Even in a spiritual sense."

"That is also the case when we use the label 'sri,' " Brahmachari explained. "As with Sri Achyut and Sri Sitaram. Sri is also a sign of respect but more in a secular manner. It is like calling someone Lord Sitaram. He is not really of nobility, but the respect is given as if he was."

I nodded my head that I understood.

"Back home, at least in the South, we have honorary titles too. Maybe you have heard of Elvis Presley's manager. They called him Colonel Tom Parker. Down South, everyone's a colonel in an honorific way. At least if they've earned that kind of respect."

"Yes," Sri Achyut agreed, "that is a good analogy."

"If you do not mind me saying," Ewa interrupted. "I mean no disrespect by this. Please forgive if I offend. But as a Polish woman I am grateful to hear all this wonderful English. I do not have to strain to listen, or to think or interpret meaning. Because of the British Empire, first with America, but now also India, and even Nigeria, we all speak such well spoken English. And even though Polish was never a part of this empire, I easily knew which foreign language I should learn first: English, because of the empire where the sun never set. As Hunter and I travelled, I would almost get an earache sometimes, trying to talk to people. No one spoke Polish, of course. I doubt anyone spoke German. But in every country someone spoke English. But it was so difficult to understand. Is that okay that I say this? Everyone now has their independence, so I can say this to celebrate my happy ears now? Yes?"

We all laughed.

"Yes, the British did much right," Sri Achyut said. "But we are all independent now for good reasons. It is time to move forward. We had our reasons for wanting self-rule, but no use to complain. Much good happened also, and here we are indeed speaking well with one another in the same mother tongue, so to speak."

"The English language served other purposes as well," added Brahmachari. "Back in Nigeria, as well as here, English, the language of the imperial power, is the unifying language even inside the country, not just of the empire. In Nigeria especially, but even here in India, there are so many dialects and tribes and regions. And if within these countries they want a unifying language to help in unifying the country, there is easily a jealousy of which dialect should be used. But everyone learns English in school, and the jealousy toward the conquering country has already been dealt with and in many ways pacified by independence. So it is easy to use that language, English, to have as a unifying language."

"That is correct," Sri Achyut said. "It was

especially bad as we gained our independence. There was such a struggle with the Muslim, who already wanted their own homeland separate from India. English made the division between groups less severe. Even in Hindu India, as Brahmachari refers to, there is jealousy with many over being dominated by the Hindi speakers. With the Urdu speakers of the Muslim population, there was even more adamancy to adopt Urdu over Hindi."

"It is ironic," Brahmachari added, "that despite the divide-and-conquer style of the British, which caused so much harm just so they could rule over us, the English language was a great unifier. And like Ewa suggests, not just within a country, but also inside the empire. And here we all are."

"The world keeps turning," I added.

"You will see the poverty in our country very close up, today," Sri Sitaram commented to get us back to the task at hand. "We have five dentists to work with this village. They volunteer their time and skill, but our charity pays for the supplies."

"Why is India so poor?" Ewa asked.

Sri Sitaram and Sri Achyut shook their heads in unison at the thought.

"Was it because of the British?" I asked.

"Some of it. The divide and conquer," Sri Achyut explained. "And suddenly much of our land was confiscated. Suddenly it was crown land. And then plantation land. Or white farmer land instead of our farmers. A subservient mindset in the conquered people."

"But India already had many problems before the British arrived," Sri Sitaram added. "Division, stagnation. The British at least opened our borders, not just to imperialism but to trade and commerce, and international banking. They brought railroads and schools. There is no one thing they did right or wrong. But what is happening now is worse than imperialism. Since independence we have had to unify, to find ourselves as a country."

"In some ways we are imperialistic to ourselves," Sri Achyut said. "Our politics are corrupt. I do not know what you know of our political system or our politicians. Some are good, but there are many not so good. I will not say who."

"And we have this vast country," Sri Sitaram came in to reinforce the earlier explanations, "with so many ethnicities and dialects. But the government wants to be the answer. It wants the power, but also to use the power to control and be the answer."

"We have families of poor that will have ten, even twenty children," Sri Achyut added further, "just hoping one will grow up and find a job and support the others. Or some of these families will sacrifice one of their children by forcefully maiming them to play for more sympathy while begging. Doctors we use have told me this, how they have to treat children that have had their arms severed just to use the maimed child for begging. You've probably seen some. If you haven't, you soon will. We have a centralized government that is socialist, except that it has no money to support the people since there are so many poor and so few rich because there is so little to our economy, an economy that taxes heavily what little it has, to feed the hundreds of millions it has little resources for. And it is the few rich we have that give to charities such as ours. If we had fewer taxes they would have more money, but also there would be more rich people and more middle class. More people to support themselves, but also to give for charity. And fewer needs for charity."

"Nothing we say," Sri Achyut said, "really explains much. The worst of it all is the subservient mentality. A subservience that began with the rigid structures of our caste system, then of colonial subservience to the British, but now to our own corrupt politicians. People beg. You will see the beggars. Who do they beg from? Millions of beggars begging from people that have little more than they have. It is the begging mindset itself that is our biggest problem."

Sri Achyut then looked directly at me.

"We need to be more like America," he continued. "Americans teach their children that they must grow up to provide. Provide. That is the key. Not to beg, to provide. It is expected in each American, beginning in childhood, that they must learn a skill, get an education, that they must be industrious. If there is failure, there is also opportunity and correction. There is an expectation to take care of oneself and to help others, not just in charity but in expectation and opportunity. All that is missing here. We beg. We beg our government, we beg our rich, we beg America, and we beg the United Nations. Even the charity of our organization with the swamiji reinforces their sense of dependency. So we must create in our citizens to provide for themselves. We have to demand of ourselves to provide for ourselves. Yet the problems are so severe, our organization is needed and cannot ignore the desperation to give charity. It is complicated. So we must do charity in our work and hope things get better."

"But corrupt politicians prevent any hope of opportunity," Sri Sitaram added further. "They are the new masters. The British are gone. Our own government is our imperialist now."

Ewa looked at me and nodded, as if to say she understood what was being said.

The van took us to a large pavilion. Hundreds of families waited in mob versions of lines, waiting on the five dentists to treat their condition. Most families wore torn and stained clothing, ragged cotton shirts and baggy pants on the men, one-piece dresses that reached the ankles on the women. As Sri Achyut and Sri Sitaram had explained, each family seemed to have at least a dozen children.

We were there all day, and still the dentists were not finished.

"We cannot just come back," Sri Sitaram explained. "We will work into the night, but once we leave, we are finished until we can arrange again to come here. Months from now, or next year, or perhaps never to this village again. If we came back tomorrow, the same people would return, even if they have been treated. There is so much to do with each patient, they will want further treatment. The worst part, I think, is the gum disease. They never brush their teeth, at least as you do with treated toothbrushes and toothpaste or with floss or mouthwash. No one has money for this. If they brush at all, there are certain trees where they tear off small limbs and rub them on their teeth as if they were a toothbrush. Some of the sap helps to clean or kill bacteria. It is depressing. Sometimes I think I cannot stand to see any more hardship. But if I do not help, then they have even less. Just knowing someone cares for them helps their lives. But also, better than me, is prosperity. When will India ever be prosperous?"

Chapter 15

"So relax," Brahmachari instructed. "Relax. That is the key to meditation. I will lead you through it. If you learn nothing else while you are here, learn to meditate. Meditation relaxes you and helps you tune in to your inner self. In practical terms, it adds quality to your life and years to your life. It helps you to get to know yourself."

Ewa and I both listened intently. I had already meditated for several years, beginning in college. I wasn't sure what all the hype was about it, and I never felt like I got that much out of it, but I gave it the benefit of the doubt. The ashram was a perfect place to learn more.

"Let's start off with position," Brahmachari instructed further. "The key is to be comfortable. It helps to have our spine erect, our neck erect, eyes closed and looking out. Let's sit on the floor now in the lotus position. Upper body erect, as I said, and then for a strong, stable foundation, sitting with our legs crossed and our feet on opposing thighs and our knees on the ground. If you've ever done yoga, or seen it done, you can appreciate this."

Ewa and I followed his example. When I meditated back home with a philosophical study group, we had sat upright in comfortable chairs. I wasn't used to the lotus position.

"This enhances breathing," Brahmachari explained. "Breathing is of the essence for meditation. But before we concentrate on meditation itself and the breathing aspects, we'll do what we can call foreplay. We'll move our heads and necks to the right in a circle, and to the left in a circle. Then forward and down, then backward, then to the left, then to the right."

Ewa and I followed his example.

"Now we are more focused and more relaxed. To gain the meditative state, we need to concentrate on our breathing. Breathe deeply in, then exhale deeply. Don't force the breathing, but we do want deep breaths. And follow your breath throughout the body. Let go of all thoughts. Some will enter your mind—that is normal— but concentrate on the breathing and it will help you detach from thought patterns that distract."

We all did so.

"Next we will do a mantra. I am sure you have heard of it. The Om. We will chant 'Om.' "

Brahmachari let us anticipate this next step to prepare us.

" 'Om' creates a vibration within us that attunes us to the cosmic vibration. Allow yourself to believe this. There is a momentary silence between each 'Om' chant. Allow the individual self to merge with the infinite self. This projects our minds past the immediate into what is inexpressible. Chant with me now."

There was a bit of skepticism inside me as I chanted "Om" with my new friend Brahmachari. I felt silly as I began to chant. I also felt silly as I sat in the lotus position. I fretted also what Ewa was thinking and feeling. Did she regret being here now?

But I trusted Brahmachari. And I did indeed come

here to experience this. I didn't have to worry about someone snickering. That was another reason I was here. I wasn't with people I considered phony, nor was I with skeptics. I was here with friends, and I did believe there was probably something beneficial to this.

I wasn't sure how long we were silent as we meditated. It seemed an eternity, and my mind wandered pathetically. I was glad that Brahmachari already forgave me, so to speak, about the wandering mind. With time, perhaps, I would get from this the silence, even the oneness we were after. But for now, my mind was wandering.

While we meditated, the same servant girl that had brought Ewa and me to our new rooms when we arrived two days ago brought in a tray of sliced cantaloupe and tea—and for me, a cup of coffee. I snuck a peek at her as she entered the room. Ewa had her eyes closed the entire time, but I was sure she was as aware of the commotion. Brahmachari seemed so entranced I wasn't sure he knew of her presence.

After lunch, Brahmachari explained, "I have studying to do. I will have to leave you two to yourselves. Sri Achyut and Sri Sitaram are gone for the afternoon. They must prepare eye doctors, who will accompany us to a village tomorrow."

"That's fine, Brahmachari," I replied. "It'll give Ewa and me a chance to walk around."

"That is good. You found your way here from Texas. I assume if you get lost you can find your way around once again."

As soon as Ewa and I left the ashram grounds for the street out front, she reached over to hold my hand. She glanced at me quickly to flash a mischievous grin. I wasn't sure we weren't breaking some cultural taboo, but I preferred to encourage signs of affection from Ewa over thwarting them, so I rubbed the back of her hand with my thumb as we walked.

"What did you think of the meditation?" I asked her.

"I tried to appreciate it," she answered. "I can understand solitude and quieting the mind, but for it to be so spiritual somehow, linked to some cosmos or something? I am not sure I get it. I will show respect, and I am here to experience other customs, but I feel awkward. Perhaps because I was brought up an atheist. I am struggling with my own religion, so it is difficult now to try to grasp another. But I do enjoy the experience."

I nodded that I understood.

"There are a lot of new age groups in America now," I commented. "I like parts of some of them. But I'm like you; I prefer my own religion. I'm lacking even in it a great deal too. But still, I do like experiencing other philosophies and cultures, as long as they aren't crazy, like child sacrifice or whatever, and as long as they are authentic and sincere. Too many people back home just rebel. They knock tradition and those that blindly follow it, but somehow they blindly rebel themselves. I guess in the overall sum total that makes sense for society. Anyway, I never got into meditation. I do it with friends a lot. I like the philosophies and dialog in this study group I belong to. They meditate too, so I go along with it. But India is the place to learn what it's really supposed to be about, or so I guess, anyway. And here we are. I hear a lot of healthy things about meditation, how it's good psychologically and physically. Maybe it's the cosmos link that we're missing. That's our fault."

We rudely ignored the beggars that flocked to us as we walked. I didn't know what else to do. I did worry that I was getting calloused about them. Ignoring them at least decreased the harassment for money.

The streets, just as in every other city in India where we had been so far, were filled with debris, filth, and excrement, both human and animal. Whole families lined the edges of the sidewalks, wearing their soiled rags, some with makeshift coverings, or roofs over their heads, held up with tree branches and sticks, as if these streets were their homes, as I was sure they were. But there were other scenes as well.

"Look, Hunter," Ewa said, pointing in front of us. "A woman dressed in her sari brings water to her home. A bucket in each hand and a vase that she balances on her head."

"That is grace unimaginable." I swooned. "It's like she's not breathing. Or even blinking. She's not moving her head at all. It's like the jar of water on top of her head is flat and secure like on a table."

Ewa looked at me to share the admiration.

"I love this place, Hunter. India is special, so special. India will be great again. She is great already, but she will be gloriful again."

Chapter 16

I watched the doctors as they worked. They were diligent, bent over their patients, who were leaned back into their long, reclining chairs. Meticulously, each doctor searched every bit of a patient's eye. Some of the patients had cataracts being operated on.

I didn't know much about Swamiji's charitable ashram. I just knew my writer friend back in Texas had stayed with them a couple of times on his visits with his Indian friend and recommended that I look them up. I'd visited my friend Jim in the Lake District of England the previous year, where he waited tables as if for old times before returning home again to finally settle down. He liked that I wanted to see the world before I settled down and told me about Swamiji's ashram, but I had given little thought to it at first. I was on my way to Israel again and couldn't see past that.

Jim kept in contact with me while I was on the kibbutz there and recommended the ashram once again when I decided to leave Israel. He arranged everything for me and forwarded a letter from Sri Sitaram to me when I got my address at the farm in Bavaria where I worked later in the summer.

And somehow here I was now. As I watched the doctors working so diligently for free, I couldn't think of where I belonged more, even as useless as I felt, and it seemed appropriate Ewa was with me.

There were so many desperate people at this eye clinic. I estimated over a hundred, all to be treated by six eye doctors. I grew up in the poorest area of America, on the border with Mexico, which was even poorer. Nothing was poorer than India, though, I was sure. I was overwhelmed, and I didn't want to be. I wanted answers. All my business courses and economic courses in college left me answerless. It was lack of answers that got us socialism, I was sure, the pure fathomless desperation one feels in a harsh world. We needed real answers—anything—socialism, religion, or whatever it took to allow us to live with ourselves complacently. But reality was better, whatever that was. I preferred the desperate questions I asked inside over answers that I knew were lies or, at best, false hopes.

"We had to turn away so many," Sri Sitaram said in frustration that night as we made our way back to the ashram.

"You cannot fault the doctors," Sri Achyut added with a sigh. "They barely took a break to eat. We will return in a month."

Sri Sitaram turned from his seat up front and looked at Ewa, who sat by a window in the back seat of the van taking us back to the ashram.

"What is it like in Poland?" he asked her. "Everything is free, so I have heard. Can you provide for everyone?"

"I do not know, really," she said as she shook her head. "My father is provided for, and his family. I have seen long lines for bread and for medical services and for housing. But I really do not know how many are serviced and how well. I have heard that many are turned away. I really do not know enough to talk much about it."

"In Nigeria," Brahmachari interrupted, "with our oil wealth, many are provided for. But still many are turned away. What will happen when the oil runs out? Nigeria is struggling to find other products or services. We are a bastion for Black Africa, but I know that many are struggling. There are many farms that are now beginning to fail. With our oil wealth, so many of the middle class and rich want imported food, especially in Lagos, where I am from. Suddenly our farmers are supplying too much food that they have no markets for. So many are starving there, especially after the war in Biafra, but many of our farmers are struggling. We need to be like Cuba. Everyone is provided for, there. Castro does not let his people starve."

Ewa looked at him and started to say something, but turned to look out the window instead. She nervously curled a tip of her hair with her finger as she did so.

"Tomorrow," Sri Sitaram said, "we go to a cotton gin. We have to take a bus for this. You are lucky in that our donors supplied us with transportation until now, with you here, but tomorrow we are on our own. We will try to solicit money from the owner of the cotton gin. He owns farms and the gin and also sells equipment. He is good at giving."

I perked up when I heard about the cotton gin.

"My first paying job," I said, "was working at a cotton gin. I grew up on a farm, but when I went off to college, since I didn't really work on the farm anymore, I helped pay my college by working at a cotton gin during the summer break. We'd work over a hundred hours in a week at times, seven days a week, no time off, up to sixteen-hour days, until we had enough cotton for two shifts of twelve hours each. So working only twelve hours a day almost seemed like a day off. I could hardly wait for school to begin again, in spite of the money."

"That's how they work here," Sri Achyut said. "And they make only the equivalent of a US dollar per day."

I flinched.

"We were the worst paid back home," I related. "Since it was seasonal agricultural work, there were no labor laws about it. We got no time and a half for more than forty-hour weeks and were paid less than minimum wage. But even then I'd get over a hundred dollars a week usually. I felt rich for a country kid. I guess I really was."

The next day we headed for the cotton gin immediately after our breakfast. It was our first bus ride since Ewa and I arrived in Baroda, but nothing about it was different.

"You must push your way on," Sri Sitaram instructed Ewa and me. "You are being too polite. You will never get on the bus at this rate."

Sri Sitaram, Sri Achyut, and Brahmachari were just behind us, impatiently waiting for us to board the bus. Even little old ladies were elbowing us out of the way to grab a place on the bus. Ewa and I could not make ourselves push anyone out of the way.

Finally, in frustration, the other three pushed and elbowed their way past the frantic crowd and pulled us on behind them. Brahmachari found our hesitancy and shyness amusing. And in all his supposed spiritual training and bearing, he was just another part of the mob when it came to the real world scenario we were faced with as we boarded the bus.

"You have to fight your way on," Sri Achyut lectured us. "You are foreigners and feel out of place to do so, but you must."

Ewa nodded her head reluctantly that she understood.

Because of our hesitancy in boarding, we cost our group from the ashram any chance of getting seats. We held on to any structure available for dear life as the bus swayed and bounced along the narrow highway that turned into a narrower, more bouncy dirt road after about thirty minutes' travel. As often happened on crowded buses and trains, some people began to puke with all the swaying and commotion. That was motivation enough for me to never again be shy about elbowing out of the way any determined little old lady for a seat on a bus while I was in India.

Before we visited the owner of the complex in his office, Sri Sitaram and Sri Achyut showed us the cotton gin itself, since I had mentioned that I once worked in one in Texas. The building that housed the gin was much smaller than those back home, and not because everything was bigger in Texas. The layout of machinery and their stations was different, to fit the economic setting.

Gins back home, primitive as they were, were almost fully automated. A person back home was needed at each suction pipe where the cotton trailer full of cotton was delivered to be emptied of its contents. And three people might be used at the bale press, where the cotton by then had been deleted of its seed and dirty lint.

The cleaned cotton was piped into the press where five hundred pounds of the lint was squeezed into a rectangular cotton bale. The door of the press was manually opened, the bale flipped onto a scale platform, then stood up on a dolly to be loaded onto a truck.

There was virtually no one else needed for labor in an American cotton gin, except perhaps a truck driver to haul off the cotton seed, or for maintenance. From the suction pipes to the spout dropping the cotton seed into a truck to the cotton piped to the press, all aspects were automated. The few laborers didn't even see the seed being stripped from the cotton boll, or the remaining lint being cleaned by a blower.

But this was not the case in labor-intensive India. People were less expensive than heavy equipment, so they were used, and jobs for them were desperately needed.

From the suction pipe, if the gin had one and did not use manual labor to cart off the cotton from the trailer, conveyer belts and levers were used to take the cotton to the machine to clean it. Each step of the way on the belt was monitored and assisted by a person, who occasionally had to hand-direct a stage in getting it to the machine.

The cotton lint was directed onto a belt to get it to a machine where a crank was manually turned for the power to separate that seed from the lint, shoved by hand or shovel to another conveyor belt, and directed on to the press. The extracted cotton seeds were dropped onto a conveyor belt and again monitored and directed by other laborers to get it to a bin, where the seeds were then shoveled onto a truck.

Child labor was often used in coordination with

adults to do these tasks. There were more skilled and educated people in India than jobs for them, but children as laborers were a desperately needed commodity in most of the Indian economy. Families would have been in worse shape without their earnings.

I felt useful when I was introduced to the owner, who was told I was from Texas and had once worked in cotton gins. I was good public relations for the ashram.

"I have seen cotton gins in America," the man told me with a smile. "Such an operation can produce hundreds of cotton bales to be processed and shipped in a single day. It is so hard to compete with American agricultural production, cotton especially. We just do not have the money for operations on such a scale. But we have many textile mills here in India, and we can produce directly for them. America has lost competitiveness with your textiles. My operation here is an industrial crumb poor countries such as ours can supply, thank goodness, because it requires so much manual labor. So what brings you here to India?"

"I had a friend back in Texas that stayed in this ashram before."

The owner looked at the others curiously.

"Jim was from Texas? Is this the one?" he asked them.

"Yes. Jim tells people about us, and sometimes people even help us because he tells them. It is good education for such as Jim and Hunter, and also now Ewa."

The man looked at me while keeping his smile.

"Jim was a very good man. He will use what he learned in India well. He was with us for a month or two, I believe. Tell him greetings when you return to

Texas. It helps everyone to share our experiences. And remember India if you ever have opportunity to help us by educating others and by support. We have so many problems."

A driver for the complex drove us all around. Most of the farm land was used for cotton, but there were also several fields with tobacco, another cash crop.

And luckily, perhaps because of my PR, the driver was instructed to drive us back to the ashram. We did not have to face the bus mob again that day.

Chapter 17

"I've read a couple of Krishnamurti's books," I explained as we sat chatting during afternoon tea. "I first heard about him when I was taking a psychology course in college."

"Yes," Sri Achyut remarked, "it's amazing how his ideas and teachings have affected the world. We here at this ashram adhere to theosophy. The theosophical society was begun in America, a creation by this Madame Blavatsky. Krishnamurti received his first inspirations as a member. He later left it. But in modern day India, Krishnamurti, in spirituality, philosophy, and psychology, is probably our biggest inspiration. It is almost a cult about him with many."

Sri Sitaram walked to a bookshelf, pulled a worn and ragged book from it, and brought it over to me to inspect.

I read aloud the title: *"The Reincarnations of Krishnamurti."*

"Take it," Sri Sitaram instructed. "Read it while you are here, and we will discuss it. This is what I mean by cult status. No one knows his previous lives, but since we believe in reincarnation in our society, and since he is so revered by modern India, this is our way to relate his bearing and meaning. In that regard, you will find it interesting."

I nodded approval that I would be glad to read it.

"I like how his subject matters include concepts of a psychological revolution," Brahmachari added. "How the nature of our minds, through meditation, inquiry, and human relationships, helps to bring about change in society, even radical change. He constantly stresses a need for a revolution in the psyche of every human being and how this type of revolution cannot be brought about by any external entity, be it religious, political, or social. That is so Hindu."

"The answer lies within us," I said while I tried to follow their way of thinking.

"It is good you came here, Hunter," Sri Sitaram said with a smile. "I am very glad that your friend Jim recommended us to you. You come with an open mind, as did he."

"It amazes me how I find this refreshing," Sri Achyut said with a chuckle. "An open mind should be the norm, not an exception to relish. I am not criticizing America or your generation of Americans, or perhaps I am, in part, but so many pass through our country looking for enlightenment. They should stay at home. Go to church. I am not even flattered they are here."

"What he means to say," Sri Sitaram broke in, "is that they are not here for enlightenment at all, but at best they seek a cult or a form to follow, like groupies at a rock-and-roll concert."

"It is worse than that," Brahmachari said. "It is like some big party. It is their ego."

I wanted to put forth my take on this aspect, but thought it best to let them talk unswayed by me. I wanted their originality about it.

It felt so good to have an uneventful day. As much as I wanted to see details of India and the operations of the ashram, to have a day off, to have no obligations, felt glorious. And with this uneventful day came yet more to see about India, with the nice talk we had about Krishnamurti, and about my American generation as seen by them.

"I have to meditate and then study," Brahmachari told us as we walked back to our room after the tea break in the main building of the ashram.

"I was going to take a nap," I informed him. "It'll be quiet for you, if you don't mind having Ewa and me in the room."

"I have a study room in another building. You two can enjoy time together. Everyone knows you won't cause a scandal," he said with a laugh. "Just to be sure, you know, in case someone comes into our room, Hunter, it is probably best you sit in two different chairs like you have been doing up to now."

"We understand," Ewa replied.

We'd had occasional private moments of temptation before. Times like now, when we were left to ourselves in our bedroom area. But to keep having them felt like we were tempting the gods. It was quite challenging to behave ourselves.

"We're going to Bombay in a week or so," I mentioned to Ewa once we reached Brahmachari's bedroom. "I heard them talk about it. There is some millionaire there who helps fund their operations. Sri Sitaram mentioned to me that they are going to bring us along."

Ewa looked at me as if waiting for me to finish my thoughts.

"Is there a Polish consulate there?" I asked her. "It's one of the major cities. Probably there is one."

"It sounds like you want me to check about my father," she answered. "To see if he has put out a search for me. Is that why you brought this up?"

I nodded that it was.

"Hunter, even if there is a consulate, I do not want to go, just in case the worst has happened. I do not think my father is in a panic about me, but I do admit I have concerns on my own that he may. I will go when I am ready. I do think about my future, but while I am thinking on this, I am living my life with you, a very, very happy and fulfilling time in my life. If my father were to be in a panic, there is a chance the Polish Embassy will not let me leave their grounds. An embassy is that country's domain. They have legal rights to do this, and India could not stop it. India would not try to stop it anyway, but they could not stop it. So I will go back home when I am ready. Somehow all this worries you. Please do not concern yourself."

"I have to worry about you, Ewa. Our situation is so complicated. And I love you. I love you, and I may not ever see you again someday because our life is so complicated."

With that she rushed over from her chair to embrace me tightly. She then released her embrace just enough to be able to kiss me deeply. After the kiss, I pulled her slightly to sit on my lap.

"It feels so good to release feelings around you again, Hunter. Just for a moment. Give us just a moment, and I will return to my chair."

I rubbed the back of her neck affectionately with my fingertips.

"What are we going to do, Ewa? What are we going to do?"

She shook her head; she didn't know. We held onto one another for several minutes, just stroking each other's neck and cheeks with our fingertips as we did so.

"What would it take to get married, I wonder?" I asked her. "What are the legal problems with all that? An American and a Soviet Bloc citizen."

She pushed back enough from our embraces to look at me.

"I love the thought of marrying you," she said. "This is what I have wanted in my desires inside. I just did not know if you wanted this too. We have known each other barely a month. I was ashamed I had such desires for you. And what to do about things if you did feel like I did. It seems so impossible. But I do not really know about the legal aspects. I am afraid to find out."

"What are we going to do?" I repeated.

She wrapped both her arms around my neck and held me cheek to cheek. After one more kiss, she returned to her chair.

"I'm going to take a nap," I said to her as I got up from my chair to lie on my bed. "I'll need the time to process our feelings and worries as much as from being tired. Sleep does that, thank God."

She nodded at me approvingly as I did so, then got up to retrieve a book from the bookshelf on the wall by the bedroom door.

"What are you reading?" I asked her as I closed my eyes to nap.

"The Bible," she replied. "I know we are here to learn from another culture. I will do so, but also it has inspired me to learn more about my own. I need the comfort as I do so, anyway."

I opened my eyes to look at her and smile, then closed them again.

After my short nap she was still reading, and so intensely she didn't notice that I was waking up. The creaking of the bedsprings as I sat up got her attention. She looked up from her reading to smile at me. It was a calm, reassuring smile that put me at ease.

I began my own reading on the book of Krishnamurti's fictionalized past lives. Soon the door opened and Brahmachari walked in. Our two peaceful and innocent faces brought out a smile in him.

"You also study," he said approvingly. "Very good. This ashram is a good place for such. We all derive inspiration."

He glanced at Ewa and noticed her book was the Bible. She saw his curious look.

"I know I should probably be reading from Hindu, or even Jain or Buddhist books," she said in an apologetic way. "But being here and exposed to all the different philosophies made me more curious about my own. How it relates and overlaps, but also the depth of my own and what I think I know and understand about it."

"Believe it or not," Brahmachari replied, "this makes sense to me."

"I will also read this book on Krishnamurti's past lives," she assured him. "And even some of his writings."

"We are soon going to a Hindu temple," Brahmachari said. "We will be using the grounds of one of the temples tomorrow to distribute food. We try not to deal so much with food charity. There are so many poor that we prefer to help only the poorest. It is often hard for us to turn those away that are also hungry, but not desperately so. We also want to break the mindset of dependency with even the most desperate. It is an epidemic here. But still there is so much need here, we feel we must at least help out in food distribution also. At least some. So we will supply some fresh fruit and also dried fruit they can take with them. Even some cheese for full animal protein."

"Does that mean we're taking the bus?" I asked.

Brahmachari let out a laugh.

"Yes, it does. We will see if you fare better on finding a seat this time. Follow the lead of the rest of us. If we can fight our way onto an overly crowded bus, perhaps you two will also be so inspired."

And indeed, it took all our will for Ewa and me to push and shove our way onto the bus the next morning. Sri Sitaram, Sri Achyut, and Brahmachari were focused but emotionless as they made a path for us. It was simply all in a day's work for them to make their way past the piranhas trying to get on the bus all at once. It reassured us we didn't have to be cruel to obtain our needed objective. We were very motivated to find ourselves a seat.

A Brahmin priest dressed in a white robe-like shirt that hung down past his thighs greeted us at the temple.

"Another fat priest," Ewa whispered to me as we followed the others into the temple. "Have you noticed every priest we have seen until now is overweight?"

I giggled slightly and nodded, though I hadn't thought of it before.

"Idols," Ewa whispered. "I am not complaining. I understand, but still this is the first time I have seen things so openly."

"Is it okay with you?" I asked her.

"Of course. I am happily here. I will not worship them, however, but I do want to try to understand the culture that produced them."

The Brahmin priest took us to the back of the temple, where hundreds of ragged people waited.

"The food has arrived," the priest told us as he stopped in front of dozens of carts of both fresh and dried fruits. "We have volunteers who will help us distribute."

The priest looked at Ewa and me and smiled.

"Our friends from America I have heard about," he greeted.

We smiled an acknowledgment and let stand his comment that incorrectly identified Ewa's origin.

As the scores of volunteers took crates of food to the intended recipients, the crowd turned into a mob. More volunteers went out to the masses of beggars to try to keep the food distribution from being overwhelmed.

As the food supplies diminished, those that already had a portion were led out of the temple grounds. Other supplies were brought out into varying parts of the yard to thin out the masses still in mob form.

Because the volunteers had limited the number of beggars, there was more food than recipients. This extra was taken out to the street and given at random to the homeless there.

As we walked to the bus stop to return to our ashram, beggars followed us to ask for money. Sri Achyut had a bag of peanuts that he threw at them in disgust. I saw the contempt he felt for the beggars. He noticed me looking at him.

"It is an epidemic," he apologized. "An epidemic here. I sympathize with the desperation. I am desperate to help relieve some of that desperation. But I do not sympathize with the engrained dependency."

Just as he said that, a well-to-do-looking family walked up to us and handed out business cards. They were dressed in fine clothing. The business cards explained that they were also beggars, as if it was a trade for them.

"There are so many ways the people beg for money," Sri Sitaram explained as he shook his head in dismay. "If they were so inventive in their ways to beg, can they not find some means at all to support themselves, or even to contribute to their own welfare? Then, as bad as our economy is, it would somehow be better."

Chapter 18

"Ahmedabad is only an hour from here," Sri Sitaram explained as we rode the bus along the way. "There is a wealthy industrialist there. He is in textiles. He is very generous to our ashram. We will visit with him and his family for two days. Though Sri Achyut and myself are not priests, we will also have religious services. It is a reciprocity we perform at times. When Swamiji is with us, he is indeed a priest. It is better. But sometimes the rest of us must fill in."

The mansion where we arrived after entering the city was huge. I had no idea just how big it was, since it was so tall and spread out. The rooms, including the ones for those of us from the ashram, were luxurious, with large comfortable beds with box springs to support regular mattresses like one would find in America and Europe. Every room we saw of the mansion was painted, with no peeling anywhere. It was the first time I had seen such well-kept structures and grounds in my stay anywhere in India.

Soon we were introduced to the owner of the mansion and textile company. To me, he was a young man for such wealth and responsibility. I was told he was only thirty-eight.

"I hope your travel was satisfactory," the man greeted us. "Welcome to my home. Make yourself at ease and enjoy yourselves. I have much business to attend, but later this evening we can dine together and get to know one another."

The man left us as abruptly as he'd arrived.

"This man's father marched with Mahatma Gandhi," Sri Achyut told Ewa and me. "Against the British for independence, I mean. Do you know anything about the independence movement?"

"I've read quite a bit about it," I answered. "Satyagraha, nonviolence and all, civil disobedience, things that Martin Luther King, Junior did later that he patterned from Gandhi, sort of."

"That is right," Sri Sitaram said. "This man's father was on the march to the sea to gather salt in violation of the British tax. Salt is a necessary element for survival, and it is free for the taking in Dandi, which is on the ocean. The British taxed everything, but to tax the salt in the ocean seemed despicable. Seventy-nine satyagrahis marched with Gandhi the almost four hundred kilometers to collect this salt and violate the unjust British law. So the father was one of those seventy-nine."

"Tomorrow," Sri Achyut explained further, "we will visit an ashram where sometimes Gandhiji stayed. They have a museum and memorial to him there. We will visit this to learn. I am sure you will enjoy it."

"Yes." I swooned. "Thank you. I love that."

Our rooms were all adjacent to one another, for convenience. After a couple of hours I heard a knock on my door.

"Hunter?" It was Brahmachari. "We'll take a quick bath before the evening meal. After that we will have a small worship service in the garden temple. A bath is a ritual, if possible, before such a service."

I went to the door and opened it to speak directly with Brahmachari. Ewa, from curiosity, opened her door to listen also.

"When your bath is complete, and your change of clothes, go to the lobby near the entrance to the mansion. It's straight ahead past that hallway, in case you forgot. Try to be there within half an hour. We'll meet there and then go to the dining room."

As Brahmachari turned to leave us, Ewa and I looked at one another for the sense of reassurance of our feelings. It kept us content during our private time until supper.

"I do much business with America," our host said as we ate. "I have direct contracts with many companies there. Also England. We are still a member of the Commonwealth of Nations, so we can have direct business dealings. The trade arrangements are very good."

"Ahmedabad is prosperous, for Indian standards," Sri Sitaram explained. "And until recently it was the capital of Gujarat. That is the state Baroda is in."

"They were telling me about your father," I said to our host.

"Yes, yes," he replied. "My father was a great man. I am very proud of him for all he accomplished. Not just for his business acumen, but in our fight for independence."

"My father fought in World War II," I said. "He was a bomber pilot. I know that involved violence, but still I'm proud. I don't know how else we would have conquered the Nazis."

"Oh yes, I understand," the host said. "Peace was possible with the British, but even Gandhiji knew the

Nazis would have slaughtered us all. Gandhi would have been the first to be martyred. Any resistance would have been ruthlessly handled by the Nazis. It was quite a challenge to stand up to the British, but yes, your father did the right thing to fight, even violently, against Hitler."

I appreciated his approval.

"We will gather, now that everyone is finished eating," he continued, "and go to our garden temple. Would you like to share our worship with us?"

He looked at both Ewa and myself as we sat next to each other.

"Sure," Ewa answered, nodding her head. "We very much would like to learn from one of the world's great religions."

"Thank you," our host said with an appreciative smile. "Can we go now? First we will wash our hands at the fountain in front of our small temple, then remove our shoes. Sri Achyut and Sri Sitaram will guide us through a small worship and discussion, along with our initiate Brahmachari. Is that agreeable?"

Ewa and I nodded as we got up to leave.

We followed our host to his large backyard garden. It had many fruit trees, flower bushes, and vegetable plots. In the center of it was a small granite Hindu temple with many carvings. In front of it, as he had explained at supper, was a fountain with a small pool for ablutions.

After we washed, we entered the temple, which was the size of a small two-room house back home.

"Do either of you know any Hindu mantras?" Sri Achyut asked Ewa and me.

"I've heard that Hare Krishna one that George

Harrison of the Beatles did," I replied.

Everyone shook their head that they didn't know. I began to chant:

Hare Krishna
Hare Krishna
Krishna Krishna
Hare Hare.

Everyone's but Ewa's eyes lit up in recognition of the chant while they joined in.

"Yes, that is a very nice mantra," Sri Sitaram said afterwards. "It was good that the Beatles came to India. It created much interest in our culture and religion."

"Here is another," Sri Achyut said. "It is to Lord Shiva. Hinduism is a polytheistic religion, as you know. For a monotheistic Westerner, it is perhaps awkward, if not blasphemous, to consider. The best way I can explain is for you not to conceive of many gods as much as to understand the psychology inside the spirituality. These gods are all just different manifestations of truth. It lets us concentrate on one aspect at a time rather than trying to encompass one large universal outlook all at once. Each has its own particular concentration."

"So," Brahmachari interrupted. "Let me lead us, if you don't mind. Here is the mantra to Lord Shiva. He is the destroyer and the transformer. Not to kill sadistically for the sake of death, but for the sake of a creation, protection, and a transformation. Death is part of life in this regard, a cycle. He is a destroyer of doubt and obstacles. Here is my favorite mantra for Lord Shiva."

Brahmachari stood rigidly and respectfully with his eyes closed and hands in prayer as he began to sing:

Jaya Shiva Shankara
Namami Shankara
Shiva Shankara Shambo.

The others began to chant with him. The words and melody were easy, and soon I was able to join in as well, and then Ewa also.

"Very good," Brahmachari praised us.

"I will explain aspects of our religion to our guests," Sri Sitaram said while looking at our host, who nodded acceptingly. Sri Sitaram turned again to Ewa and me to continue. "Hindus believe in the four *Puruṣārthas*, which are the proper goals or aims of human life. These are *Dharma*, which is ethics and duties, *Artha,* which is prosperity and work, *Kama*, which is desires and passions, and *Moksha*, which is liberation, salvation, and freedom. There are also *karma*, which are actions with intentions and consequences, *samsara*, which is the cycle of rebirth, and the various yogas, which are the paths or practices to attain moksha. Some Hindus, such as our Brahmachari and Swamiji, leave their social world and material possessions in order to engage in lifelong sannyasa, which is to live monastic practices to achieve moksha. Hinduism prescribes the eternal duties, such as honesty, to refrain from injuring living beings. We prescribe patience, forbearance, self-restraint, and compassion, among other things."

"To sum it in a nutshell," Brahmachari added with a chuckle.

It amazed me how so many of the so-called great religions and philosophies overlapped. There were definite differences, not all of them good, perhaps, but many were related, even if customized.

The next morning our host arranged for a van to take us to the ashram nearby, where once Mahatma Gandhi stayed. Since Gandhi was a key historical world figure from modern day India, I felt fortunate to get a guided tour of his movements.

The ashram was a simple one, made up of locals, for the most part, living in cottages on the grounds. There was also a small pottery factory and a few textile looms. Our ashram in Baroda seemed to have some kind of link with them in a way I didn't fully understand, but all of us there from Baroda were asked to speak after we arrived, not just Sri Achyut and Sri Sitaram but also Brahmachari as well as even Ewa and myself. Perhaps hearing from other parts of the world was uplifting to them. At least it provided me a way to help pay back our ashram.

I studied the manner in which our ashram leaders spoke to the crowd. Both Sri Achyut and Sri Sitaram gave short, to-the-point talks of encouragement. Brahmachari, however, went into a long, elaborate spiritually based talk I assumed was meant to be uplifting. There was no way I was going to do anything like that. I also wanted to set an example for Ewa to follow, in case she felt shy or in the dark about what to say.

"My whole life," I began my talk, "I heard of this great soul and great saint, Mahatma Gandhi. I cannot fully take in the significance of being here with you today to say something to you. Mahatma Gandhi was not just one of the foremost leaders for your country, but all throughout the world he set an example for all of us to follow. I have read much about him. Here at your ashram you undertake self-reliance. He emphasized spiritual strength, but also self-reliance. India is undergoing many struggles. There wasn't just political struggle against the British in Gandhi's day, there was struggle for self-reliance, whether through cottage industry or anything else. That is still very important today, even with independence. Independence also means freedom to fail. We all must find ways of success. I wish you well in the spirit of Mahatma Gandhi. Many of you may well know that recently in America there has been much political struggle. A man named Martin Luther King, Junior used Mahatma Gandhi as a major example of how to succeed not just by political struggle but, more importantly, by basing it on inner strength and moral truths. America is so grateful to you in India. As an American, thank you for providing us so much insight."

I got polite applause from the audience. I wasn't sure how much they had understood of what I said, or if it was routine speech-making they thought they heard from me. But my ashram companions made prominent displays of encouragement to me for it.

"That was very well done," Sri Achyut said. "Short and sweet. And very significant words. Thank you, Hunterji."

"That was wonderful," Sri Sitaram praised. "It makes our struggle here feel appreciated. Even in our downtrodden state, it is a reminder that we have contributed to the world."

"Great speech, my ashram friend," Brahmachari said.

Ewa winked at me, then nervously walked to the podium for her speech.

"Good morning," she greeted. "I come from a

place in Europe you may never have heard of. From a country that has been conquered many times and at times not even existed. It exists today only on paper. It is ruled by tyrants. Mahatma Gandhi faced strong opposition with many days in jail and beatings from a colonial power, but at heart, a civilized one. There are tyrants in the world that are not so civilized, but the longing for freedom against them is there in my country. It is God given to long for freedom and self-reliance. A brutal tyrant named Joseph Stalin took over my country after World War II. The world watched it happen. While India was gaining independence, my country was vanquished by an atheist who slaughtered tens of millions of his own. Would a Gandhi work out successfully in my country, then? I am here to tell you that this same man, Joseph Stalin, once laughed when he mocked with the question, 'How many battalions does the Pope have?' To him, only brute force maintained power. But now the Pope is from my country. He is free and mocks, through spiritual strength, the tyrants that rule Poland today. And through God, and Pope John Paul II as his earthly liaison, we will again be a free nation someday soon. And as I speak to you now, there are trade unions in my country that are inspired by what they saw in the country where I stay now—your country, India—and its saint, Mahatma Gandhi, its guide. Your courage and your strength is there for us to use for our own independence. I cannot express to you the pride I have to absorb all you have done for the world and, in particular, my country. Thank you."

Ewa then put her hands in a prayerful gesture, bowed ever so slightly toward the audience, and proclaimed, "*Shanti*, shanti, shanti. Peace, peace, peace."

The ashram stood and cheered her as she walked back to us. Traces of defiance remained in her eyes as she looked at me for approval. I grabbed her hand as she approached me, then kissed her on the cheek. The others with me rushed to hug her.

"You are wonderful!" Brahmachari exclaimed.

"You make us so proud," Sri Achyut said. "We pray for your brave country, my dear."

"It is so wonderful to have you among us," Sri Sitaram praised.

Chapter 19

Fundraising was as much a function of the charitable ashram as spending those funds on projects for the poor. Since I witnessed firsthand the menial living conditions on the ashram, I could not doubt the devotion behind spending those funds. It was not for themselves the ashram existed. Putting up with the bus rides alone brought home to me how cheaply these men lived in order to provide for the poor around them. And watching this same devotion helped minimize any judgment I may have cast toward Sri Achyut and Sri Sitaram for the disgust they displayed toward the beggars that haunted them as we walked the streets of Baroda. All the desperate poverty these men had to deal with day in and day out surely drove them to make their own jobs obsolete. This disgust toward beggars, I determined, was the only outlet they had in which to deal with all they faced.

Bombay was a five- to six-hour train ride due south of Baroda. We were going to see yet another millionaire textile owner—and for the first time meet Swami Subbaraya. It would be business mixed with spiritual matters once again.

Ewa and I were tempted to ride on the top of the train, just for old times, but this was an express train, and the others in our entourage secured seats for us.

"So why are you here in India?" I asked

Brahmachari in front of the others as we travelled. I was surprised at myself that I had never bothered to find out until now.

"I was brought up in a Christian church within the British colony of Nigeria," he related with a grin as he brought back the memories. "Between this being the religion of the imperial power, as well as seeing all the religious strife from the civil war we had between Islam and Christianity after the British left, I suppose I was dissatisfied enough with things I saw. I met Swamiji a few years ago when he visited the Indian community in Lagos, my hometown. I was very impressed."

"Swamiji," Sri Sitaram broke in, "is looking to have an ashram set up in Lagos. We have contacts now, but we would like something more solid. Brahmachari is one of our initiates. He is very educated and responsive. So we are working together toward that end."

I nodded at the explanation.

"I am glad you have the chance to meet Swamiji," Sri Achyut added. "He will spend time with you. We have much business at hand, but he will be glad to include you in talks and our services while we are there."

"We will be in Bombay for three days," Sri Sitaram said. "You and Ewa will have much time to walk around the area of the mansion where we will be staying. There is a beach nearby, also. That will be nice for you. And you can talk with Swamiji."

"Be sure to show him the respect for a swami," Brahmachari instructed.

"How do you do that?" Ewa asked.

"It is best to kneel and then lie face downward,

prostrate," Brahmachari explained.

Everyone saw how I flinched at the thought of doing that.

"But if you have problems with it," Sri Achyut said, "just give a simple bow, with your hands in a prayerful manner."

The mansion where we would stay was the biggest yet, ten stories high, and luxurious. It even had an elevator. With all the high taxes in India, how much money did this family make to still have money for this?

Even though there were so many guest rooms, Brahmachari and I still shared a room, but a room much like a suite in a luxury hotel. Ewa had a room all to herself next to us. It was just as large and just as luxurious. I never wanted to leave.

The dining room, where we met the owner hosting us, was like a grand ballroom. The owner was elderly but very alert and energetic.

The saffron-robed Swami Subbaraya was also elderly and had a shaved head, with quite protruding earlobes and eyebrows. Even as he politely smiled our way, he exuded an air of command in his demeanor.

Immediately, upon meeting him, all from our ashram lay prostrate before him, even Ewa. I just could not bring myself to do so, however. But I did make a slight bow from the hips, with my hands brought to a prayerful pose, as I was instructed.

"You are the American?" Swami Subbaraya asked me straightforwardly.

"Yes, I am, Swami."

"What brings you here?"

"I am a friend of Jim from Texas. He was very

impressed with your work and recommended you to me."

"Yes, Jim. I remember him. A fine man. Very scholarly. How is he?"

"He's doing great."

Swami Subbaraya then looked at Ewa, who was now standing up once more.

"I have heard great things of you. And that you are from Poland. We are most pleased to have you with us."

"Thank you, Swamiji. I am so excited to finally meet you."

It wasn't long before several Brahmin priests entered the dining room. All were dressed in white trousers with long white blouses that reached halfway to their knees. And all were, as Ewa had brought to my attention earlier, somewhat chubby, unlike our rather slim Swami Subbaraya.

Every vegetarian Indian dish imaginable, I assumed, was at our disposal. I remembered my boyhood visions of what vegetarians had to endure since they were not allowed to eat meat. I didn't care now if I ever had meat again. The dishes were marvelous. I recognized potatoes, rice, beans such as lentil and garbanzo, and of course tortilla-looking morsels of bread. I had no idea what else was in these recipes, except of course curry spices.

The owner, our host, sat at the head of the vast, feastlike table. Swami Subbaraya was to his right, but it was Swamiji who was the center of attention. Everyone came to see him. Just who was this guy? The word "swami" itself sounded important. And everyone made a big deal of our swami. He seemed more important than I'd imagined. If someone spoke to him, he answered in short, deliberate sentences. When the others spoke, it was somehow wrapped around Swamiji and his duties.

"We will go to the temple now," Sri Sitaram instructed us as everyone got up from the table to leave.

I assumed he meant a temple outside the compound. Instead, it was a temple that took up the entire top floor of the ten-story mansion in which we were staying. We took the elevator to it.

Swamiji spoke to us there. That's what everyone wanted. He led the mantras, he spoke philosophy, and he led the rituals and prayers. When he finished, the service was finished, and we rode the elevator down to the second floor, to a den-type area.

"Would you like to step outside onto the balcony?" Sri Achyut asked Ewa and me.

"That would be nice," Ewa answered.

A servant followed us and opened a door for us.

"Bombay is so huge." I gasped as I looked at all the buildings and houses around us.

"Yes," Sri Achyut concurred. "We are in the more affluent area. But nearby the vast slums begin. They extend all the way to the beach on the Arabian Sea."

"So, it's the Arabian Sea that's here," I said.

"Yes. It is not a far walk. Perhaps you two would like to see for yourselves, in the morning. I will give you a business card just in case you lose your way."

"Thank you," Ewa said with a smile.

"Look there," Sri Achyut called out as he pointed to the sky. "Do you see them?"

"See what?" I asked.

"Do you see a ways in front of us these large birds

flying and circling?"

"They look like vultures," I said in disgust.

"Yes, yes, Hunter. Yes, that's exactly what they are. White sacred vultures."

"Sacred?" I asked.

"Yes. Do you know of the ancient religion of Zoroaster? From ancient Persia?"

"Yes," I answered.

"This religion has no home anymore. I mean no home base. They are scattered all over the world now, but in such small numbers. Bombay is their home base in exile, you might say, since they were driven out of Iran by Islam. They wandered here through the centuries, especially after the Muslim conquest of India. Those towers there where the vultures fly, those are the sacred towers of the Parsi religion. Parsi is just like saying Persian—the Persian religion, as in Zoroaster. That is their major temple in the world now, the building in front of you where the vultures fly. There are only about a quarter million Parsis left here now, from what I understand. And these vultures that are flying mean that someone just died. For a Parsi burial they lay out the dead body after a day of waiting for friends and relatives to be notified. Then the body is put to rest openly in a tower, and the white sacred vultures are released."

"Wait a minute, Sri Achyut." I gasped as the reality of what he said sank in. "Are you saying these so-called sacred vultures are released for the dead body of the Parsi? This Zoroastrian?"

"Yes. They are left to feed on the corpse. After a few days, someone goes to check on the body to see if there is anything left. When it is just the skeleton, the bones are left to bleach and then are broken up and entombed."

Ewa and I looked at one another, ready to die. Every bit of nauseous emotion was expressed on our faces.

"It is a natural way, Hunter. It is their way of returning to God."

I looked frantically at my hands. My beautiful, wonderful hands. Hands I never wanted to part with in my sentimental Jewish way. I had no idea if there was really a resurrection of the body someday, like the Pharisees of old indicated. I even doubted it. But boy! I loved the thought of my body easing its way to God on its own without any help from pyre fires or sacred vultures. Why it mattered was beyond me. But suddenly, it did matter.

That seemed our cue as Ewa and I made our way outside to walk the nearby streets of Bombay. It was my first time to be alone with her for two days. Even in this more prosperous neighborhood, the streets were filthy with debris and excrement. And there were once again so many homeless beggars.

"Oh, my goodness, Hunter. Look into the street directly in front of us. Do you see?"

I did as she instructed and saw what she was pointing out. In the middle of the street was a man lying down, with cars zooming all around him. It was as if he had some death wish. Would it do any good if I ran out and pulled him onto the sidewalk? Why weren't others doing something to rescue him? I waited and never saw the break in the cars I needed to drag him in. Would it do any good? Would my act of kindness give him a boost to want to live, or would he just go back to the street to await death? How were these cars missing him? How long had he been there? No one paid this scene any mind except Ewa and me.

Finally, I walked out into the street to stop traffic. Horns honked, but one man stopped to pull the body into his car and drove away. I never found out if the body was alive or dead.

To calm ourselves as well as reward ourselves, we used this incident as an excuse to openly hold hands as we continued our walk.

"Hunter, see ahead," Ewa said with a smile, as we walked to pet one of the Brahma cows walking the sidewalks with us. The cow patiently let us stroke her until we began to walk again.

Soon I began to smell the salty air, which now was strong enough to overcome the foulness and smog around us.

"I see the beach up there," I said to Ewa, pointing at the gap where the ocean began, approximately a block away.

As we arrived to walk on the beach, we saw the excrement, both human and animal. A few yards beyond us, in the middle of the strand between the ocean and the street, was a woman squatting to relieve her bowels. Ewa and I held hands all the more firmly while we continued our walk, trying not to notice the woman.

"At least the skyline was pretty," Ewa commented as we returned to the mansion where we were staying and rang the bell for the servant to let us in.

We were noticeably shaken by what we had seen in one of India's most prosperous cities. By now, we should have been used to scenes such as we'd witnessed, but somehow we never would be.

Instead of a servant, it was Brahmachari who answered the door to let us in. He looked concerned as he motioned us to enter.

"I have news for you," he said. "Let's have tea in the den."

Ewa and I looked at one another curiously as we followed him. He remained solemn the entire time, until finally we sat down on one of the couches beside a table with the tea and fruit prepared for us.

"We had a visitor while you were gone," Brahmachari explained, "from the Polish Consulate in Bombay."

A chill rushed through me. I looked at Ewa and saw nothing but fear.

"I'm not sure how he traced you here, Ewa," Brahmachari said while looking her directly in the eyes. "This isn't Poland, and they have no secret police here. But they know you're here, somehow. Or they know you came here. I lied to misdirect them, but there is trouble brewing. I just hope I bought you some time."

Ewa began to nibble at her lower lip as she listened.

"Someone from the Polish embassy in New Delhi went to our ashram in Baroda, looking for you there. They were told we all came here, to this address. So the consulate here sent people for you. I'm not sure what they wanted, really, but they asked if you were here. I told them that you went with an American friend of ours to an ashram in Pune. That's a couple of hours from here. That is another one of those ashrams for hippie types to get enlightened. I said you two wanted to check it out. He asked when you were returning here, and I said I was under the impression that you weren't coming back here, that you were going to Pune and might stay a while. I hope that will send them on a wild goose chase for enough time. Plus there are so many Americans and Europeans there that maybe they will get confused in their search for you."

"It was my speech in Ahmedabad," Ewa replied solemnly. "That's how they knew I was here, I am sure of it. My father knew I was going to India overland with friends. I did not tell him where. I did not even know for sure where we were going, actually, or when we would arrive."

Brahmachari began to nod his head.

"That is what Sri Achyut decided," he concurred, "that your speech about a free Poland was so stirring that some began to talk about it. And somehow the right person heard about this Polish girl at a Gandhi ashram talking about a free Poland. It is a long shot for it to reach someone that would bother to tell the Polish Embassy, but maybe not all that long a shot. You wouldn't need secret police for something like that. And if your father put out a search for you through the embassy and consulates here, any hint would be checked. And low and behold, a Polish girl right here. How many are there that are not assigned to India somehow? Not many. Then how many at an ashram from Baroda that visited this famous ashram in Ahmedabad?"

Ewa looked at me, desperation in her eyes.

"What choices are there for me now, Hunter? I am not ready to go home. I want to spend more time with you."

"What do you want to do?" I asked her.

She shook her head at me, showing her doubts and fears.

"I have part of the answer with me now," Brahmachari said.

He reached into a pocket and pulled out an envelope and handed it to her.

"They left these," he said. "That doesn't mean they didn't believe my story about you going to Pune, but they know that we are a contact for you."

Ewa opened the envelope and read.

"This is an airplane ticket," she explained holding it up. "An Aeroflot flight for January third. Today is December twentieth. That is about two weeks from now. There is a letter attached. I am to fly to Warsaw. If not, on January fourth my passport will be revoked. I have physical possession of it now, of course. They can't cancel it if they can't find me, but they can cancel it on paper and on the computer. It will have a detrimental effect even if I have possession of my passport."

"Sri Sitaram and Sri Achyut are talking to Swamiji about this," Brahmachari said. "Maybe they have a plan. I don't see how they can help you, really, but we need to think and talk and make some kind of plans, depending on what you feel you need to do, Ewa."

She nodded that she understood.

With that, we went to the library on the third floor, where our ashram patrons were.

"Swamiji," I said as I entered the library, "I hope you have the authority to perform marriages. Because I'm going to marry Ewa, and I hope to do so today. Ewa has to fly out of here by January third or they cancel her passport. Marry us. Help us."

Swami Subbaraya let out a laugh.

"My dear fellow," he said with a gleam in his eye. "The Marines have landed. Yes, I have authority to perform wedding vows, but Hunter, you would have to register. And actually, I have been discussing just such arrangements with Sri Achyut and Sri Sitaram— contingency plans, as you might call them. We are very aware of the strong feelings you two have for one another. But let me explain the complications with this contingency plan. For the two weeks that Ewa is here among us, it would be a legal marriage. But by January fourth she would be a woman without a country. Or at least a passport."

"Then she can come with me to America. As my wife and as a refugee."

Swami Subbaraya laughed yet again.

"I so admire the spirit of Americans. Especially Marines. The can-do attitude. But let me explain reality to you. She is still a Polish citizen. She is not a refugee. Her life is not endangered, as far as we can tell. Her father is a prominent figure with the Polish establishment. They just want her back. She abused her privileges and must be dealt with. Not in a threatening way, we must assume. At least that is how the American government will look at this. She will not qualify as a refugee."

"But she's my wife," I said defiantly.

Swami Subbaraya shook his head no.

"The status of intermarriages between NATO countries and Eastern Bloc countries is that if such a marriage is challenged, it is null and void. You can be married here, but even India could not recognize this marriage if it was challenged. For two weeks you can be married as long as it is not challenged. It will be challenged very quickly. The father will see to it, and so will the Polish government, for that matter."

"Then marry us so that we can be married for two weeks," I insisted.

Everyone turned their attention to Ewa.

"Yes, Swamiji," Ewa replied emphatically, "marry us even for two weeks. Let it be so."

"My dear Ewa," Swami Subbaraya said softly with a sigh. "I will be glad to perform such a measure of love between you two. There is a thirty-day wait period after you register, however. And you must register with your embassies."

Our hearts sank. None of this surprised us, but it hit hard anyway.

"First," Swami Subbaraya continued, "let us get past the heat of the moment, as they say. Tomorrow is the winter solstice, and we will escape to an ashram an hour's travel from here. It is in a village located in a rainforest. That is what we, Sri Achyut and Sri Sitaram, have decided is the best thing to do in the short run. We will be driven there by our gracious host. I talked with him this morning, explaining the situation. He will provide us a van and driver, and we can go on a retreat there. But my advice to you is to take your ticket. Face your consequences. Work with your situation and move forward. I can imagine you will not be allowed to leave Poland again, however. You must be aware that is possible. Actually, I would think it is probable."

Chapter 20

What India called a village, Texas called a small town. The ashram where we were taken was part of a village surrounded by a thick rainforest where seven thousand people shared their lives with tigers, lions, monkeys, birds, and other rainforest creatures. It was indeed a retreat, the perfect place to try to figure out what to do with a crossroads-of-life decision.

The structures in the village were primitive but sturdy and clean. We came upon no beggars. Whatever it was that people in this village did, they found ways to support themselves. No one looked especially poor. It was as if the rainforest filtered out dire poverty. Nor did anyone look particularly rich. The dwellings were mostly wooden; even if made of stone, they were small, two- or three-room structures.

There was a small stone temple inside the ashram that was open to the entire village. Swami Subbaraya led services for the village when he was present. It being winter solstice, there was a celebration and service for the darkest day of the year, light to bring enlightenment.

All of this perked Ewa and me up. We sensed our fate, but for now we had strength to enjoy what time we had left together.

"Swamiji," Ewa said as we returned to our quarters on the ashram after the solstice service that night. "I have something to show you."

She brought out a scrolled piece of paper from her backpack and handed it to him while standing next to him ready to explain it.

"This is a marriage certificate presented to Hunter and myself in Vienna. I am not asking you to violate any law in India, or any protocol of your religion, but Hunter and I have only a short time left together. May we be married during our last days here? I wish not to cause anyone problems, but please take pity on our situation."

Swami Subbaraya studied the piece of paper in front of him. In Polish, it meant little to him, though he did see seals from the embassy.

"See," Ewa continued, "it indicates in Polish how we are married."

Swami Subbaraya studied Ewa in sympathy.

"How did you get this certificate, Ewa?"

"We knew we would be travelling together and wanted few complications about our arrangements. Many countries and cultures are very strict."

He eased into a smile.

"Is this legitimate, my dear?"

Ewa hesitated. "You see the seals, Swamiji."

"Yes, I do. Yes, I do. But what will you do with this now? It won't stand up to international law. I told you that already. Or even Indian law."

"But you mentioned the thirty-day waiting period. The registration we have to do. This is from two months ago. Hunter and I would just like a small religious ceremony to make sacred our life together for the next two weeks."

Swami Subbaraya began to nod his head. He turned

to look at Sri Sitaram and Sri Achyut. They likewise nodded their heads. Swami Subbaraya then put his arm around Ewa.

"Ewa, you have blessed us beyond measure with your presence among us. You have risked your freedom and status to be with us and jeopardized everything for what I was told was one of the most stirring, heartfelt speeches honoring our country. I will be glad, right now, in our sacred temple, on this winter solstice, to make sacred your vows of matrimony to our beloved Hunterji. And were it to be challenged and found not binding in legal terms, I can assure you that it will never be questioned by the sacred."

A tear rolled down Ewa's cheek. She immediately hugged him and placed her head on his shoulder in endearment. Swami Subbaraya was noticeably moved.

It was late, but all in the village who were still awake were invited to attend the Hindu wedding ceremony at the temple for the purpose of our sacred marriage vows. Ewa wore her dress and dress shoes. Swami Subbaraya used no books or notes as he gave the sacraments for Ewa and me to follow. Brahmachari sang sacred songs before and after the vows.

And we were married. A signed certificate of marriage, handwritten by Swami Subbaraya in the Sanskrit script of the Hindi language, was presented to us.

"We have a house for you," Sri Achyut told us. "It is for special guests when we have special events. You are the most special guests, and this is a most special event."

It was a two-room wooden cottage on the edge of the ashram grounds. One of the rooms was a bedroom with two single beds inside, wooden-framed beds, with a mattress on each. We immediately pushed the two beds together as we had often done on our travel overland. The memories we intended to make together in these next two weeks would seal us and, if need be, get us through the rest of our lives.

All throughout the next morning, villagers came to our cottage bringing well wishes and food. We wanted to go out and walk through parts of the rainforest, but we were so touched by the kindness we waited until we were sure no more visitors were coming.

"Do you hear the screeches?" Ewa asked as we walked a path leading from the village that afternoon.

"No idea what they are," I said. "Guess we shouldn't wander too far."

I then looked at her as we walked.

"Are you happy?" I asked her.

"Hunter, I cannot imagine how my life could ever be more fulfilling. I am scared to think of the future, but all that has happened gives me courage beyond measure. I will make it, Hunter. I will survive anything that happens to me when I get back."

She rubbed my cheek with her fingertips, and we stopped walking to kiss.

"It gives me courage too," I said. "I will be worried sick about you, but we have all of this. It gives so much strength."

"There is fate, Hunter. You do understand that. Fate. We are fulfilling our fates. I can take anything else now in my life, knowing fate has placed us together."

I nodded yes, absolutely yes. I believed in fate.

We had been asked to be back at the ashram by

midafternoon. In our retreat, Swami Subbaraya wanted to instruct us in Hindu philosophy. Ewa and I both wished to hear him talk anyway, as part of our experience in India. But especially now we wanted to share with them their foundational beliefs, to pay them homage for all they had done.

Swami Subbaraya sat with us outside the temple, under the shade of a large tree in the middle of the ashram. He sat on the ground with his legs crossed, in the demeanor of teacher to student.

"The most important characteristic of the Hindu world view," he instructed, "the very essence, in fact, is the awareness of the unity and mutual interrelation of all things and events. It is the phenomena in the world as a manifestation of oneness. All things are seen as interdependent and inseparable parts of a cosmic whole. In other words, different manifestations are of the same ultimate reality."

"That is where karma comes into play," Brahmachari noted. "Why an interrelationship creates this cause and effect."

"Yes, Brahmachari. You have studied well. You have good understanding."

Swamiji looked at Ewa and me.

"The universe is dynamic, then, in this interrelationship. It moves, it vibrates, and it dances. Eastern mystics see the universe as an inseparable web with interconnections. All are dynamic and not static. The cosmic web is alive; it moves and grows and changes continually. Therefore, everything we do has significance."

"Like my speech at the ashram that now has me having to go home," Ewa remarked.

"Yes, that is an example," Swamiji said. "But what caused this stirring speech from you, Ewa? The conditions in Poland. Even Stalin, decades ago. It is an endless cycle. And your returning now will cause more interrelation. Remember this, Ewa dear. We are all here for you. We are a part of you. Be with us as you deal with your conditions and realize they also will cause reactions. It is important that you handle this well. You are human; you may not handle everything in the purest manner, but remember this: if you feel anger, there may be a good reason. It may even do some good, but it will have a reaction. I hope the peace and love you have received here can give you strength and guidance to uplift even your antagonizers."

"I am ready, Swamiji. I know I will struggle, but I feel so prepared."

Chapter 21

It was Christmas. Though Ewa was the only Christian in the ashram, everyone celebrated with her.

"Thank you so much, everyone." Ewa swooned toward the many well-wishers around her. "My very own Christmas tree! Or bush. I am glad you didn't uproot it. Now it will continue to grow, and you will remember this day with me. I love your decorations— popcorn, candles, flowers for wreaths. I am so touched and happy. And I have yet another excuse to wear my good dress and shoes."

"No Christmas goose," Sri Achyut joked. "But we have a Gujurati favorite that perhaps will suffice for your Christmas treat. It is called *Ubadiyu*. It is a delicacy made of vegetables and beans with herbs."

"And wonderful Indian spices," Ewa said. "I am so happy. Thank you all so much."

"And best of all"—Brahmachari gleamed— "Christmas carols. I still remember many of them from my youth. And our American here, even though he's Jewish, surely knows many."

Brahmachari and I, for the most part, led the charge in singing along with Ewa. But there was always a chorus of some sort by those in the village who knew at least parts of a few.

"This is the greatest Christmas of my life," Ewa said with a gleaming smile later that afternoon as we strolled along yet another rainforest path. Her hand was swinging in an exaggerated, jubilant manner as she held onto mine. She looked at me as she did so. "Actually, this is the grandest time of my entire life. Living in primitive housing, riding filthy, overcrowded buses, nearly getting killed by a mob in Iran, getting diarrhea." She let out a giggle. "And meeting you."

"Good to know I'm right up there with diarrhea," I said with a chuckle.

"Yes." She laughed in return. "Right up there. Oh, Hunter, I am so unbelievably fulfilled and happy. All the consequences I must pay for this happiness and for releasing my feelings in a speech honoring Mahatma Gandhi is all worth it. A lifetime of adventure, growing, and endearments in my two months with you. I will survive anything now."

I looked at her, showing the concern I felt.

"Do you mean that?" I asked.

Her demeanor turned more serious.

"Yes, I do. But I admit, it takes courage. I am frightened by what awaits me, Hunter."

"What do you think is going to happen? We only have a week more together. Then you go back."

She shivered at the thought.

"I know. It haunts me. Leaving you haunts me, just the thought, and leaving our friends here at the ashram. It is a whole new world and culture I have been allowed to experience, and so much devotion that I never dreamed possible. But leaving to face the uncertainty— I admit it frightens me."

"What do you think is going to happen?" I repeated.

She shook her head.

"My father is angry with me, I am certain. But he loves me. I will talk with him. First I will hear what he has to say, to gain his thoughts, to see what he knows or thinks he heard, and perhaps his fears of my desires. But the authorities? Yes, them—that is a different story. They may bear down on me. If I can assure my father, he can help defend me, but he is not so powerful. Just influential."

"They don't know anything, Ewa," I instructed her. "They didn't send out agents. There were no news reporters at the ashram to hear your speech. Your father put out some kind of search for you through the embassy when you wrote him from Vienna. Probably he just wants to talk to you. Probably he was bugged that you went off with an American like you did instead of staying in Vienna preparing for studies. He may not even know you went off with an American. Let him tell you what he knows. If he knows for sure you went off with an American, he'll tell you. You don't have to lie, but you don't have to admit it. You can include that you also came across a nice American and he was interesting. Things like that. Dilute the truth. If you lie outright, you may get caught in a web. But you can dilute it or not even mention it. Use your judgment. But I guarantee you they don't know what you said in your speech to the ashram. What came back to the Polish Embassy is that a girl from Poland gave a rousing speech against tyranny. They don't *know* you did, they *heard* you did. Here's what you can say. Unless you're set and determined to go down as a martyr for the cause, back in Warsaw, say this, and live to fight another day. Or live to live another day. Simply say that you were inspired by being on one of the ashrams of

Mahatma Gandhi. And in that spirit you mentioned Stalin and how many battalions does the Pope have. And now there is a Polish pope. And he was inspired by the spirit of Gandhi. If you say that, Ewa, and nothing more, you can make them think the rest is all hype and rumor. Do this. Don't be a martyr."

"I wish not to be a martyr. I am glad you think about all this. This is very good advice. Yes, I will consider what you say. I do wish to make it up to my father, and I also wish to regain my freedom. There are things going on now in Poland, like I say, with the trade unions and with the new Polish Pope. I do not need to be a petty martyr used for propaganda purposes by the politburo establishment. I do not need to embarrass my father, who has been so good to me and given me so much freedom. I do not want to make him regret that more than he already does."

She squeezed my hand approvingly.

"What will you do after we leave here on January second to return to Bombay and take me to the airport the next day?" she asked.

"There is an old Jewish settlement in Cochin. That's south of here, near Goa, the former Portuguese colony. I want to talk to some of the descendents there, and see some of the tropical part of India along the way. Then I guess I'll go over to Sri Lanka from there. That's a Buddhist country. It used to be Ceylon. You probably know that. Anyway, it's another country and culture to see. And from there I heard you can get dirt-cheap flights out of Bangkok, so I'll probably fly there after Sri Lanka and buy a packaged trip back to America. I heard you can teach English in Hong Kong, and in Taiwan, even South Korea, and Japan. I want to see if any of that is true. If the worst happens, I have my ticket home. But if I can support myself at all, I can travel more and experience more."

"Oh, and you will do all of this without me. What glorious plans you have, Hunter! I want so badly to go with you, but we have different journeys in our lives now. So, alas."

"You need to memorize my Texas address, Ewa. Go ahead and have it written down somewhere, but memorize it so you can write it down again once you get to Poland. And if the worst happens, you have friends in Vienna. Is there any way you can sneak letters to me through them from Vienna? Do you have friends at the Austrian embassy in Warsaw?"

"Hunter, you have so much concern to stay in contact with me. This touches my heart. Yes, I can do all you say. We will find each other again. I promise you this. You are the love of my life. These are not just pretty words. You have given me the happiest and the most fun days I have ever lived. The deepest, too. You won my heart. None of this will go away as just some fancy time."

She looked at me for emphasis.

"I do not know how you feel, Hunter, but I can tell you, I have two pieces of paper, one of them sacred, that I am your wife. And I am. I am your wife. Totally. Someday we will marry for real. The legal one. The one that says I will never say good-bye to you again. Do you feel this way? Is there any hope of this from you?"

We stopped walking and turned toward one another.

"You are my wife. Forever my wife. Yes, things are happening in Poland. I will wait for you. I promise you this. I will wait for you. Never ever lose hope. If we lose contact someday, never ever lose hope. I will wait for you. Do you understand that? We will find each other and somehow get around all the legal obstacles. We believe in fate, right? We were meant to find each other now, to do all we have done, and to complete that fate together someday."

I wanted to make love to her right there in the rainforest. We hugged and vowed words of love yet again.

Chapter 22

As the time for leaving the ashram approached, Ewa became more and more restless. Every event, however trivial, became something to cherish, to cling to for meaning, to hold on to as some kind of anchor. It felt like cheating to sleep, wasting time that needed to be spent on memories.

"You're reading the Bible more," I commented. "Swami Subbaraya's talks don't help?"

"Of course his talks help, Hunter. Nothing has changed. I did not realize I read more from the Bible now. I am trying to find my balance, I suppose."

"Is everything okay with you, Ewa, now that we have to leave soon?"

"It is so wonderful here in the rainforest, at the ashram here, with Swamiji, with you. It all is giving me something—structure, spirit. Yes, I need his talks and I need my Bible. I would want this anyway, but to go home, I need it even more."

"What is it you're reading in the Bible that's helping you?"

"Jesus did not just accept things, did he? Life was not just a list of do's and do not's. He was not being a skeptic so much as he was searching."

"Like you."

"Even more than me, but yes, I identify in my way."

"I love that about you, Ewa."

"I remember what you told me when we first began to travel," she said with a smile. "How you liked this about me. How you saw me as a searcher."

"A seeker," I corrected.

"A seeker," she concurred. "You told me how seeking was important even more than believing, that questions were just as important as answers."

"Never change that, Ewa. Never stop this search you're on. You're beautiful when you read the Bible. I wish you could see yourself. I totally melt. You are this person who saw Vienna and wondered why Warsaw wasn't like that. It spurred something in you. You have a seeking soul or you would never have cared. The Bible was meant for people like you. And you're going to need that search when you get home, while you're waiting to marry me someday."

"I am married to you now. But I know what you mean. Yes, I will need this search to get me through until we can be together again."

"Keep reading the Bible while you wait."

"Sri Sitaram gave me this Bible. He wants this to be the Bible I read in Warsaw."

"Perfect," I said.

"Besides, the Bible is for everyone, Hunter. I appreciate that you approve of my search, but the Bible is for everyone. It is what keeps my people in Poland alive."

"The Catholic Church does that," I commented.

"What's the difference?"

"I like the Catholic Church, and you need it. You need the support group, too. But your search is different, even if some of it overlaps. Too many people, including Catholics, only follow."

"That is what God wants."

"God wants seekers," I told her. "And if you don't listen to Swamiji as a seeker, or read the Bible as a seeker, you're just an ornament of God, not a follower."

"I am not sure what you mean," she said.

"As a Jew, one of the things I have a problem with in the New Testament is the portrayal of Jews. How we were all just a bunch of legalists back then. Jesus was a Jew. I don't mean that was his religion, though it was. So many Jews back then were past following a bunch of rules. But that's all you get out of the New Testament. A bunch of legalistic pinheads enforcing the law. Such legalists did exist. But Jesus, the Jew, one of many to do so, wanted more. So many Christians today are legalistic pinheads even as they quote about the legalistic and morally corrupt Pharisees. So you are so refreshing to me. You seek. You look for meaning, so deeply. I don't know if it's because you were an atheist and need these answers you are now finding, or if you're that way instinctively. So many Christians just memorize the Bible."

"What is wrong with that, Hunter? I memorize the Bible, just like I have memorized your address in Texas."

"Yeah, but you memorized my address so that you can find me with it. Same with you and the Bible. Go ahead and memorize the Bible. As long as it helps you find God's address. But so many memorize the Bible and don't have a clue what it means. Many memorize to assure themselves they are on the right path, or to spit out passages at somebody someday. You can memorize the Bible, but you can't memorize God."

"You are a guru." She laughed. "You should stay on the ashram. Forget about Bangkok."

"I am happy here. But Bangkok calls. My journey through life while waiting for you calls."

And then it arrived: New Year's—joyous, ominous New Year's. A new year, but the last day at the ashram.

We had another walk on a rainforest path together, another session with Swamiji and members of the ashram. And then, as was now custom, we took in our favorite village scene, watching the wives and mothers walk from the village well, carrying jugs of water in both arms and perfectly balanced on their heads. Harmony.

And then it came nightfall—our last night together before returning to Bombay.

The joy in the village was exuberant on this New Year. Ewa and I both forgot ourselves in the celebrations. How wonderful to absorb the festive mood. The entire village was awake that night, with music, a feast, even fireworks. There was no room for dismay, and it reassured us.

****

Somehow Bombay looked more prosperous as we returned in the van our host once again provided. There were still beggars crowding the streets, still excrement on the beaches, and still smog hovering in the skies. But people made their way to the marketplace, to jobs in the shops and offices, and to temples to give fruit to the gods. If Bombay still had spirit, if India had survived so many setbacks, there was going to be prosperity again someday. It already had the history, the wisdom, and the cultural momentum.

"Congratulations are in order," our host told Ewa

and me as we reentered the mansion. "I heard the wonderful news that you two are married. Swamiji told me it was the happiest occasion of any marriage he has performed. I wish I could have been there. We will feast it now. Come to the dining room. Our last day together will be our happiest."

Silverware and fine china were set out on the tables. Extra tables, in fact, were brought in to accommodate hundreds more guests, including many from our host's factories. The finest foods were presented on silver trays. Even a small musical ensemble was present to play classical Indian music.

"One day," our host said as a toast to Ewa and me, "we will have yet another feast, upon the return of our friends that we honor today. Until then, stay vigilant. What is meant to be will happen. And we will know why it was important to walk the path set before us."

Chapter 23

I will wait for you, Ewa.

That's what I told her as we parted at the Bombay airport in early January 1979. That's what we had to believe.

And there was no other choice for me. I loved her.

I had a letter waiting for me when I returned to Texas several months later. It arrived in April 1979, and luckily my mother put it away in a safe place until I got back home.

"I am sorry, my dear husband," it began, "that it took me so long to write you. There were many complications and very much to explain to my father. My father was very angry with me, but in a loving way. I got him in very much trouble. Yes, suddenly, his daughter that he trusted ran away with hippies overland to India. He could not believe I would do this. Such Western decadence, and coming from me. He did not know I was with this gorgeous American Marine that I would soon marry. He thought me so irresponsible. But not so irresponsible like I really was in going with you. Better a bunch of hippies than an imperialist Marine, I am sure. Then it is like you said. Some Polish girl in some ashram from Mahatma Gandhi gave a treacherous speech about the evils of her worker's paradise country. How could it be possible? No one from the embassy would dare do that. Maybe some Polish girl from

America that pretends to be a victim, but is instead an American hippie or something. There were people from the Polish Embassy in Ahmedabad while we were there, Hunter. They heard of my speech a few days later. An Indian businessman they met heard about my speech when he visited the ashram, and he told them. Then these embassy workers go back to New Delhi and there is the search document from my father looking for me. Maybe this is the traitor. This girl that runs away from her father. So they find from the ashram in Ahmedabad that there was a Polish girl with an ashram in Baroda. That's why they think I ran away with hippies. Our ashram in Baroda was a true ashram, but so many hippies seek enlightenment that they go to ashrams made for hippies and the Polish embassy does not see the difference. And so they sent someone to our ashram in Baroda and got the address in Bombay, only to find I ran away to yet another hippie ashram in Pune. That is funny, but that is the only part that is funny. My father was incredibly angry with me. But I told him what you said to say. That surely, my wonderful father, you understand that I would never ever doubt you or our wonderful worker's paradise of Poland. I simply was giving a speech to people about Mahatma Gandhi and how he stood up to the imperialistic British, at the same time that Stalin, who no one pretends to like anymore, invaded Poland. And so I convinced my father I meant no harm by it. That somehow people needed to think that a poor Polish girl victim, me, is trying to escape tyranny. Even after my father believed my story, he remained angry because he knew he had to face the police and convince them. And to say to them my daughter ran off with hippies. I told my father I was wrong to leave Wien, but these hippies were going overland, and the appeal was so big for me that I could not resist. Finally, the police believed my father. But even though they did not revoke my passport, they took it back. I am not allowed to return to Wien or leave Poland for a while. So I had to wait to write you, my husband, until I knew my fate. Please notice my address. It is in Warsaw, but that of my best friend. She is of the proletariat, and I can trust her. I was so happy to read your letter from Taiwan where you found a job teaching English. I am glad I gave you my friend's address in Wien. She forwarded to me your letter from Taiwan. What excitement it gave to me. Write me, my husband. I have memorized your address. I also left a copy of it with my best friend. Never lose faith, my love. We will meet again. Fate awaits us. We will be married again. I love you."

When I finally wrote Ewa back, it was months before I received a reply. She was studying music in Cracow. Her being in Cracow made it easier to write, except that I also was moving around. All we could do was every few months write a letter of assurance. It was even dangerous to write very often, for fear someday our liaison would be discovered.

Once we lost contact with one another. That was frightening. That occurred in 1985, after a full six years of being apart. My parents had moved, and I was living in the Philippines. Ewa's letter to me was forwarded to my parents' new address, but not for over a year. The people living where my parents used to live held the letter, then misplaced it, only discovering it a year later before forwarding it. I did not see that letter until months later, upon my return from the Philippines. Ewa was frantic by then, especially with all the new events happening in Poland.

Even before the Berlin Wall fell, which symbolized the breakup of the Warsaw Pact, Ewa got her passport back, and with the turmoil in Poland preceding the breakup, managed to leave in 1988. We met in Vienna. We had never lost faith.

"You're still so beautiful," I said to her as we hugged at the hotel where we rendezvoused for the first time in ten years.

"You lie so well, my husband, but I want to believe you. I know I have gained weight, and I have lines appearing at my eyes now."

"You haven't gained much weight. And we're both still in our thirties. We can have children."

"I am a tourist," she fretted. "Poland is falling apart politically, but I am not a refugee."

"But we can get married. I can get you a fiancée visa. It won't be challenged."

"How do you know?"

"I don't. I'm just judging the times."

"Where will we live?"

"Texas. I still have my job with a university that I told you about in my last letter."

Ewa looked up at me as if finally allowing herself to feel secure.

"I cannot pretend I never lost faith," she said. "Actually, I never did, but at my worst I had grave fears. But I can tell you what got me through. Your vow to me that you would wait for me. You meant it. You loved me, and it was not just a memory or emotion. You loved me. I had proven myself to you somehow. I could tell you meant it. But what sealed it was the love we found in India. We probably were there at their worst period since independence. They had so much to overturn and they had to find themselves, too. But their historical wisdom was still there in them. That got them through. All the love Swamiji and Sri Sitaram and Sri Achyut gave to us, and that Brahmachari gave to us, that all gave me so much foundation, and so did even the wedding feast our last day together in Bombay, and our Afghani friends in Mashhad—all these wonderful people along the Hippie Trail for us! Oh, Hunter, they all gave me strength to know you and I would find each other again. And here we are."

"And here we are," I repeated as if it were a vow.

Shortly after we got married in Texas, Poland had a new government, and soon after that it was aligned to the NATO countries.

All these years later, we know the wait only made us more sure of ourselves. There was a fate. And our fates were intertwined, one way or another. There was no one else I ever wanted, even when I feared I would never see her again.

If we had not gone overland together, or not gotten married at a temple in an Indian rainforest, we might surely have lost desire through the years. However this stuff works, it works when you're listening. The wait for ten years only seemed part of our marriage. An interlude, but a marriage, nevertheless.

We have three beautiful children to show for our marriage, two strong boys and a girl even more beautiful than her mother.

We never made it back to India. Swamiji died a few years after we left, and the ashram broke up soon after that. Ewa and I still intend to go back someday anyway, maybe after the kids are grown. But India is prosperous again, and we want to see it. How could it be otherwise?

We will need to fly to India if we ever do return. The Hippie Trail is fallow now. The Shah of Iran fell shortly after we left India. The mullahs there are hostile, and it would be foolish to tempt our fate by passing through that country. But even worse is the state of the Khyber Pass and all the kidnappings there. As dangerous as the world seemed back then, it seems a bigger mess now.

But whether we visit India again or not, I still listen to Beatles songs that sometimes place me back there emotionally. And now I write stories about all I've done, too. None of my stories matter more to me than the one I just finished. The story of how I met the love of my life in Ewa. How a girl from Communist Poland ended up spending the rest of her life with me. But that's how fate works. I'm here to assure you of that.

A word from the author...

Born on October 7, 1948, in Harlingen, Texas, where I grew up and worked on a cotton farm, I graduated from Harlingen High School in 1966 and attended Texas A&M beginning in the summer of 1966. In January 1970 I dropped out to enlist in the United States Marine Corps, where I served as an enlisted man, attaining the rank of sergeant, with an honorable discharge after three years. I worked as a computer programmer afterwards in Houston and as a civil servant for a US Air Force Base in Frankfurt, Germany. I traveled and worked in Europe for two years, which included flying to Israel in October 1973 to aid the Jewish State in the Yom Kippur War. I was also in Greece in the summer of 1974 when the war between Greece and Turkey erupted over Cyprus. I was stuck on the Greek island of Ios for part of that war, until I managed to catch a boat to Athens just in time to watch the Greek military dictatorship fold. I returned to Texas A&M in the fall of 1976 to finish my bachelor's degree in Business Management. I returned to Europe afterwards and also to Israel, where I lived for almost a year. I later taught English in Taiwan before returning home in 1980 to get a master's degree in Agricultural Economics, received in 1982. I joined the US Peace Corps in 1984 and served for three years in the Philippines. In 1987 I began work for the Swiss government as a computer programmer until 1998. I have worked in the IT department of Texas A&M since 1998. I have three children and am presently divorced. I am Jewish.

Thank you for purchasing
this publication of The Wild Rose Press, Inc.

If you enjoyed the story, we would appreciate your
letting others know by leaving a review.

For other wonderful stories,
please visit our on-line bookstore at
www.thewildrosepress.com.

For questions or more information
contact us at
info@thewildrosepress.com.

The Wild Rose Press, Inc.
www.thewildrosepress.com

Stay current with The Wild Rose Press, Inc.

Like us on Facebook

https://www.facebook.com/TheWildRosePress

And Follow us on Twitter
https://twitter.com/WildRosePress